On the
Surface Tension

By
Dietrich Biemiller

Printed in the United States of America

ISBN 0-9975915-4-5

Biemiller LLC
PO Box 425
Lake Stevens, WA 98258

www.biemiller.net

Dedicated to The Late Bloomers,

The Overlooked,

The Overworked,

and The Undervalued

—PROLOGUE—

The flying yacht *Golden Wolf* was a SkyGalleon Model 42, top of the line, tastefully appointed and worth every penny of the $300 million that Ron Golden had paid for it. He would have been disappointed to know that, as they were cruising through the Cascade Range, it was about to be steered into the side of a mountain at 400 miles per hour.

Ron was unaware of this. So were fellow passengers Tracey Springs, the LaGrue twins, and Jack Strong. They sat around a table before a large glass window, motionless, frozen mid-word. The crew of thirty also had no knowledge of the danger. This was because the entire craft, the air it was flying through, the mountains, and the universe beyond was frozen in time. The Mods had hit the pause button and the world had stopped. A Steward carrying a tray of water glasses was stopped, mid step, the water from the pitcher he was pouring transfixed midway to the glass. A fly that had managed to stow away was suspended mid evasive action from an attacking swat from the purser in the corridor to the head. The Chef, in the galley, was petrified in the act of pulling a tray of seared scallops stuffed with fig, walnut and Gorgonzola out of the oven, the smoke stilled mid-swirl. The pilot's hand rested a foot above the control stick, still curled as if it was gripping it.

There was no sound, but for two breaths, belonging to an unusual looking man and woman at the bridge of the yacht. They alone were awake, aware, and present in the stillness. They stood slightly askew from the deck, like they were manifesting into the space imperfectly but well enough. The thin bald man in a well-tailored gray suit and tie pushed his round glasses up the bridge of his nose and gripped the flight control stick after moving the pilot's hand, looking ahead of the craft for an appropriate surface to steer the ship into.

The somewhat overweight woman in the blue dress with her hair sticking out of a contrived hairdo in weird directions placed her hand on his arm.

"Wait," she said simply.

We discussed this already, Duma," he said, but removed his hand from the stick nonetheless.

"I know, Barman, but I am changing my mind now that we are actually here."

"What has changed?" he argued. "The situation is the same. This entire story has gone completely off the rails into lunacy. One day we had a guy eating his breakfast cereal and then he's the richest guy in the world. He's off to Neverland fighting the immortal devil sponge surrounded by zombies, pirates, ninjas, aliens, gunfights, laser beams, A-bombs and talking octopusses. This is something straight out of the Hell universe line, not the way it is supposed to go in the mundane line."

"Octopi," Duma said, "Yes, but it isn't their fault. It is all due to the ripples from the decision that Eiffelia made."

"You know our job. We are Moderators. We observe, we keep the story going. We keep the grand bargain, and that sometimes means doing edits with a light hand."

She barked a laugh. "Flying into a rock wall is hardly light handed. I get it that it solves the local problem of stretching the ground rules to the breaking point, but it does nothing to solve the Eiffelia problem. Let's let them play it through. If they succeed, it's back to normal with a good story enjoyed. If it keeps going on this trajectory..."

He made a sour face. "I still think right now is the time to do the stepping in. I don't think they will resolve the Eiffelia problem without even more bleed over from the Hell universe line. You give them enough rope and they will still hang themselves."

Duma raised an eyebrow. "So we are at an impasse? Then there is only one solution."

"Gah," Barman spat. "This looks bad on us if we have to involve an Admin. They solve the present problem but it complicates our ongoing progress. We have worked together a long time since having to call one in to resolve a conflict. What was it, the Sumerian spiritual expansion with Enmebaragesi the Lugal of Kish problem?"

"You forgot that business with Constantine and the battle of the Milvian Bridge," Duma corrected.

"Oh. Right. Forgot that one. Anyway, I would prefer to resolve this without higher intervention."

Duma shrugged, and wandered from the bridge to the main saloon where the passengers were seated. Barman followed, curious. She regarded them in turn.

"She has just gotten under way with her Trident career, it would be a shame to crash her into a mountain," she said.

"Ah, but without the Eiffelia business there would have been no need to make such drastic changes to the fabric of the story," Barman countered, raising his finger. "No Trident, no silly Pangborn Genes, no underwater tribes of refugees, no galactic level war."

"That might be true, but there is some inherent flexibility in the surface tension of the universe that has not yet been ruptured. No thanks to those little scamps," she said, pointing at the LaGrues. "In spite of them, I think we can allow the other passengers of this craft to try to regain that normalcy without - you know, crashing them into a mountain."

At that moment a small point of light appeared in the saloon, shining brightly.

"You called an Admin?" Barman accused with exasperation.

"Not me," Duma protested.

"I came on my own, hearing the conflict," said a disembodied voice. "How to manifest? This looks like a ship, so I'll be a Captain."

A woman appeared, dressed in an elaborate navy blue uniform with a feathered captain's hat, jeweled buttons, gold fringed epaulets, and a brass and leather spyglass held in place on her face by eyeglass frames.

Barman and Duma exchanged glances. "She's worse at playing human than we are," Duma whispered.

"What, this is wrong?" the woman said, as the spyglass-glasses fell by their own weight from her face.

"Welcome, Administrator Anpu, to the *Golden Wolf*. Duma and I were just discussing our ongoing monitoring of this world line, there is no need for you to intervene. Unless of course you feel that you do. Which you must, since you are here. Obviously."

Duma rolled her eyes.

"Let's see, let me catch up," said Anpu. "Correct me if I go astray. Bifurcated main universe lines, one freeform and one hardcore. Current main subjects are humans, which are bipedal mammals who habitate the lines called 'Hell' and 'Earth' respectively, and reproduce by..." she fluttered her hands all over her torso until they rested on the crotch.

"Oh dear. How odd. Anyway, current conflict involves one of the denizens of the freeform universe line who has illegally infiltrated the hardcore mode while retaining an artifact that allows her immense power in relation to the hardcore characters. And you have stretched the normal hardcore mode by infusing normal characters with abnormal training and experiences in order to restore the order."

"Yes, that is pretty much the story in a nutshell," said Duma.

Admin Anpu pursed her lips and nodded. "Who is that one?" she asked, pointing at Ron.

"That is Ron Golden," said Barman. "He is the one who was written in to have a special gene that keeps universe lines open, which was important to the escapee Eiffelia who manifested as a relatively immortal species of sponge. Once she got into the war with those guys," he said, gesturing to the LaGrue twins.

"Do they know it was him yet?" asked Anpu.

"Not yet," answered Duma. "He hasn't stolen the rift generator yet and started duplicating himself to start the war. That happens soon."

"And who is that?" asked Admin Anpu, indicating Jack.

"That is Jack Strong," said Barman, "just another guy who happened to have the gene. He got roped in to the story by getting recruited by a super-elite team of government Space Command and FBI and CIA and Trident guys who ran a secret underground base reverse engineering a starship that crashed from the war and opened a rift into an alternate universe line and discovered flying pickles and pirate tribes living underwater and blew up part of the sponge by using an atomic weapon to trigger an underwater mud volcano ...and, uh...yeah," he petered out as Anpu gave him a withering glance.

"How did you two allow things to get so ridiculous in a common hardcore universe line?"

"Well, there was some bleed over," explained Duma.

"I see," said Anpu crisply. "And this woman, I presume, is the one who is being trained to actually accomplish this restoration of the two lines?"

"Indeed," said Duma. "That is Tracey Springs, and she is being developed to be one of a group who act as our agents from within the universe line, since our direct actions are disruptive. This group is called 'the Trident,' and include Adrian Smithson, Maurice Drew, and Andrew Morrow."

"Oh, I remember Andrew Morrow," said Anpu, perking up. "I've watched him since he was an insect. I suppose this universe has its good points. I shall consider this before I decide whether to erase it or not."

Barman and Duma regarded each other with alarm.

"Erase it?" Barman asked, a tremor in his voice. "I thought the decision was whether to let things proceed or crash the craft into the rocks."

"The problem is more fundamental, my dear Moderator," said Anpu. "You know how many universes are stacked in the Library of Souls. Here they would liken them to a vast library, stacks as far as the eye can see. All created by the developer, administered by us, moderated by you Mods. This..." he gestured around him, "is but one of them. They don't all work out. Once a world goes off the rails we must give consideration to pulling the plug."

"That would be rather drastic," said Duma.

"Are you worried more about this world or of your reputation and development as a Moderator who has been unsuccessful?" Anpu asked.

Duma resisted the temptation of arguing, and considered the question honestly.

"That had not occurred to me, and while it may be an underlying personal concern, the prospect of losing an entire interconnected series of universes and all the attendant lives connected to them is enormous in comparison."

"No lives would be lost," observed Barman. "They would all proceed with other stories in other universes.

"Yes, but the investments!" countered Duma.

"Investments in what?" Barman countered. "Certainly not time, since the real universe runs beyond the space and times of these library book universes."

"It is the investments of their stories, of course," said Anpu. And of course if the stories have degraded beyond a certain point of quality, it is our responsibility to turn off that particular movie or tv show or video game. But I do observe that there is a waiting list for entry into this universe line, and this hardcore mode version in particular. Strangely enough." She exhaled deeply, bobbing her head about.

"Very well," she continued. "Let's let this play out. I reserve the right to revisit this decision if things don't resolve quickly."

"So we don't crash the ship," Barman said, somewhat disappointed. "Can I at least move the stick a bit and leave the Pilot's hand in the air? The resultant lurch towards the mountain might serve as a wake-up call to the players."

"Very well," said Anpu. "I will see them all eventually, one sooner than later."

She vanished.

"I wonder which one," said Duma.

—1—

"You promised a meeting to go over this whole 'alternate universe' thing you have been going on about with Jack Strong," Tracey demanded. "It has been six months since you started acting weird. You have been avoiding me. So when will it be?"

Ron drummed his fingers on the mahogany table and looked out the window of the flying yacht at the terrain of Western Washington slowly rolling by two thousand feet below. His eyes followed a broken line of concrete that had once been a highway. He saw what looked like an automobile crawled along it.

"Hey wait, is that a car? I thought they had done away with those things now that we have flying cars and flying yachts and things."

"This is why I worry about your sanity, Ron," said Tracey. "Of course the Poor can't afford actual cars that fly. They just keep rebuilding the old-time gas engine wheeled cars to get around."

"Yes," agreed one of the LaGrues seated on the left across from Ron and Jack Strong at the table. "It is amazing that those who haven't the work ethic necessary to hold a job and who sponge off society to provide basic food and shelter can still have the wherewithal to find parts for those ancient jalopies and the knowledge to keep them running."

"It's disgusting," spat the other LaGrue on the right. "I can't imagine how smelly they must be with unrefined gas. I guess they can't tell how stinky it must be over their unwashed bodies and clothes. But I can't imagine why they feel the need to go anywhere to begin with. They get everything provided to them by the Owners and Workers. And they keep breeding like rats. Something must be done."

"Out of sight, out of mind," answered the left LaGrue.

Ron and Strong exchanged glances.

"I guess there is still a lot we don't know about this brave new world," Ron said.

"Enough of that," protested Tracey. When will you finally tell us about this bizarre story you have been hinting at for the past few months so we can pick it apart and bring you back to reality?"

"Right now," Ron said with a brief smile. "We have some time before we get to the assembly factory."

"Hoo boy. Here we go," said Strong, sitting beside him.

"I still think you are behind this," accused Tracey, stabbing her manicured finger at Strong. "And the LaGrue twins are with me on this, not you two."

The twins exchanged a helpless and noncommittal glance across the table.

"Well I can't convince you against your own experience of your life history," said Ron. "All I can do is lay out the sequence of events, then let reason guide you."

A white-coated waiter brought drinks and hors d'oeuvres.

"Thank you," said Ron.

"That is one clue supporting your story," Tracey admitted. "You never used to thank the help. You were kind of an asshole before this change."

Ron raised his eyebrows. "Well there you go. Exhibit One: no longer an ass."

"Well, not as big an ass."

"I'll take that," Ron said. "Anyway, so before the events preceding our recent adventures, I was an out-of-work game programmer and you worked at the Seattle Aquarium. We lived in a rental in North Seattle. You had a daughter named Chris who was a student at the University of Washington and a son named Jeremy who had just shipped out to boot camp for the Marines."

"You are already in the weeds on this, Ron, because if I had kids I would have had them in this universe too."

"Not necessarily. Obviously. Maybe things worked out differently with your ex, Dory. So anyway, right after the time when Pop died, I got this visit at the house from some government agent guys who said some face-painted clowns were going to try to kill me." He paused, waiting for the inevitable incredulous reaction from Tracey. She merely stared at him deadpan.

"Go on," she said flatly.

"So the assassin types drove by and the government guys saw them and then took us to a secret underground base under the Denver Airport where they discovered I have the rare Pangborn gene. You have a recessive. My gene allows me to keep different universe lines open. Jack has the gene too, by the way. Your gene allows you to do some kind of special things with dreaming or something—I'm still not clear on that yet. They had a crashed spaceship down there through a rift to the other universe, from some kind of galactic scale war that was going on against...well we never really found out against who. And there were flying pickles down there too. But anyway, we convinced the government types to let us go home."

Tracey took a sip of her drink then placed it on the table with exaggerated precision.

"So then of course the face-painted guys attacked. Turns out the leader of that gang, Cornish Bob, was one of my ancestors! He wanted us to join him, believe it or not. He and his little buddies were nasty, though. We got away, more by luck than anything, and decided to go back to the underground base to hide. They asked us to join up with a team made up of Special Agent Clay, a pretty doctor named Valentina Pavlov, and different versions of Smithson and LaGrue. We went with them to investigate a different rift to another universe that might have been in Bodie. And it was."

"Don't tell me we went from one made-up universe into another one."

"Well yes, in fact we did! In this one we had sea dwellers called 'Tribals' and we started to end up with them, but we got split up and captured by Eiffelia the Devil Sponge."

Tracey held up her hand to halt him. "Wait a minute. So in the first universe we had no Sea Tribes? But we did in the new one?"

"That's right!" said Ron, warming up, glad she had focused on that instead of the reference to the satanic sponge. "Which is the weird thing, because you were someone else in the new universe, a Pirate Queen. But you had died there, so you didn't run into yourself like LaGrue did."

"Well there you have it," Tracey said to the twins. "You weren't twins like you are here; you met each other as different versions of yourselves."

"Wait a minute," said Strong. "Do twins have the same fingerprints? This is one way we might be able to prove they are the same person and not twins!"

The LaGrue twins looked alarmed, then reached for their familiars to look it up.

"No," the one on the left answered. "Twins have different fingerprints. It never occurred to us to check this. But were we twins in the other universe?"

"I...let me walk through this," Ron said. You were one LaGrue in the original universe, then ran into the other you in the other universe. Then you both came back to our universe, then we had the change into the hybrid one. So I am thinking you could either be twins born here or two separate LaGrues who now have alternate memories."

"There appears to be a way to tell," said the LaGrue on the right. They both took their glasses and made distinct fingerprint impressions with their right index fingers. They compared them.

"Identical," said the LaGrues in unison. "So we are two versions of one person, not twins."

"Exhibit Two, then," said Ron.

"Please continue," said Tracey, momentarily taken aback.

"So anyway," Ron stumbled, trying to recapture his narrative, "you took back over from the Pirate Queen's life and learned how to...I think, put your consciousness into other things, like either flying pickles or a giant octopus, I don't remember which. I got away from the sponge's undersea prison, then we met Strong here and blew up the devil with a nuclear bomb with the help of Cornish Bob, my ancestor. I guess he had a change of heart. Or sides at least. I dropped him back in time so he could get away from Eiffelia too, and then when we all came back to this universe—it turns out that there were no more of the carriers of the gene in that line, just me and Strong here, and we had just left it. So it collapsed into this universe, which is now some kind of unholy combination of the two where we have Sea Tribes, flying cars, and a history where I ended up a rich guy. So there you go. Our adventures in a nutshell."

Ron watched Tracey as she mulled this over.

"It goes without saying how stupid that whole story sounds," she said.

"Which supports the truth of it," said Strong. "I mean, if we were making it up, wouldn't we make it sound less idiotic?"

"Ok, then explain this. If you were living in another universe as a game programmer and then had all these wacky adventures, then popped into existence in this universe, what happened to my husband? You know, the 'you' who grew up here, married me, ran the company? Knew about this world? What happened to him?"

Ron and Strong exchanged glances. "I don't really know. Other than I am Ron Golden and always have been. That Ron either stopped or never was, and your history with him was entirely in this universe line that only came into being when Cornish Bob made it. Maybe my coming here started another new line when the other one collapsed. Maybe that Ron wasn't a Pangborn carrier."

"Ah, if I may interject," said the LaGrue on the right. "This is quite fascinating even if unsubstantiated, but it may be possible to verify even more beyond our fingerprints. May we ask some questions?""

"Shoot," said Ron.

"If our ad-hoc fingerprint experiment proves incorrect upon further actual investigation beyond looking at smudged prints on a water glass, it would be easy to chalk this whole story up to insanity or group hysteria between you and Strong, with one exception that defies explanation. The rift generator."

"Go on," said Tracey.

"Well, think about it," said the left LaGrue. "We can confirm that there is no current technology or science that would explain the existence of this device. If it in fact does what you profess, it is indeed proof that it comes from another universe or at least a part of ours that is to date unknown."

"Have you seen it actually work?" asked Tracey. "He has been keeping pretty close to the vest with the thing, and I have yet to see him pop out of the world. As far as I know, that is all part of his delusion."

"As far as we know, that is correct," said the LaGrue on the right. "But the possibility of the veracity of the claim had been enough to generate our willingness to construct the orbital pod."

"The what?" asked Tracey.

"I would like to hear an update on its preparations before we arrive at the plant to inspect it," said Ron, rubbing his hands together in his best evil mastermind imitation.

"The orbital pod is nearly complete," said the LaGrue twin on the left. "But we still need to use the rift generator to figure out how to attach it to the pod and power it."

"Orbital pod?" asked Strong, eyebrow raised.

"Yeah, it sounds geeky, I know," said Ron, helping himself to a seared scallop stuffed with fig, walnut and Gorgonzola. "Tell him how it works, LaGrue."

"Well," began the twin on the left, as both of them warmed up into their beloved lecture-mode, "from what you describe, the rift generator works either by hand-carrying it, where it pulls everything in a small radius along with it when it jumps, or by installing it in a craft, where the entire hull of the ship can be used, even if it is really big. But without an actual ship that uses a rift generator, we do not know how the effect can translate across the whole ship."

"Okay," nodded Strong.

"So we will have to make the pod fairly small to make sure the whole thing goes with you when you jump. And until we actually get to examine the artifact you describe as the rift generator, we have only been able to construct the thing based on your reports and a visual examination. Not that we blame you for your caution in letting it out of your control. Next we need to determine where to go. From what you report, the coordinates of Eiffelia's home planet had been entered by Cornish Bob before he went back into the past and founded this empire. The choice, then, is whether to just jump to the planet surface without a ship or to use a ship and jump into orbit around it. Both have their advantages and disadvantages."

"And why are we going to the home planet of this... Coppafeelya?" asked Tracey.

"Eiffelia. To rescue your kids," Ron reminded her.

"Oh, right. My kids. What were their names again?"

"I would imagine," said Strong, "that jumping directly to the planet surface would be better because Eiffelia would likely have all sorts of sensors in place to detect things entering orbit around her home planet. Due to that big war she's in."

"True," agreed the right LaGrue, "until you realize that she may have chosen a water planet to live on, and Ron may well materialize right in the middle of an ocean somewhere. And even with gillsuits it might be weeks before they found land anywhere. Even *if* there is land."

"That would be...well, wet anyway," Strong grunted.

"So hence the orbital pod. We had to make it big enough to live out of for long enough to do some scouting, airtight and pressurized. And of course shielded as best we can from detection. We have chosen to modify a standard car, like the one we are in now, as a starting platform.   Once the decision is made to land and where the landing will be, the entry craft will be deployed. Once on the planet surface, the only way back is using the rift generator—either to go back to the orbital pod or to come directly back here. Making the craft capable of blasting back out of the gravity well into orbit would be too costly in size and weight. The entry craft is one-way only.   From the surface you will have to just jump directly back here using the rift generator alone, just making sure Tracey's kids are with you."

"And more difficult to determine," said the left LaGrue, with a widening grin, "is how the generator knows where Cambria is now and not just when Cornish Bob entered the coordinates a year ago."

"Uh, yeah, how *does* it know?" asked Ron.

The right LaGrue shook his head. "How indeed? We have no idea. I mean, we are on the Earth, which is rotating at around 1,040 miles per hour. Then the Earth is revolving around the sun at almost 19 miles per second. The whole solar system is moving through the galaxy at 155 miles per second, and the Milky Way galaxy is moving relative to our local cluster at 185 miles per second. How the hell does that box calculate one point in spacetime to another over years, let alone five minutes? That is another reason why we need some time to poke around on the actual machine, not just the gold ball portion that powers it."

"You...need to hold it?" asked Ron.

The LaGrues, as one, reached out their right hands. Ron hesitated, but pulled out the rift generator box.

"Wait, what am I thinking? We have the blueprints for you to make one of your own!"

The LaGrues were puzzled. "Where did you get such a thing?

"From my Pop! Before he died he was working on notes, and it turned out that they were plans for a rift generator. There were angels helping him, 'music of the spheres,' he said. He told me about it when I was down in Eiffelia's prison."

"Your father was in the prison at the bottom of the trench? How did he get there from our universe if he didn't go with us? Did he perfect a rift generator before he died?"

"Uh, no. He told me about it after he died."

The LaGrues squinted in puzzlement.

"You know...as a ghost. But I was insane at the time. So I guess we don't have any plans, unless he made them here."

"I strongly doubt that," said Tracey. "Your father devoted himself entirely to the company and died when you were quite young."

The LaGrues extended their hands again.

Ron slid placed the rift generator on the table. Before the LaGrues could reach out for it, the flying yacht suddenly lurched towards one of the sloping rock walls of the mountains that the ship was navigating through. The generator slipped off the table to Ron's feet. They gasped and grasped the arms of the chairs they were sitting in, and heard a crash from the tray that the Steward had dropped. The ship righted itself immediately.

"What the hell?" Tracey spat.

Ron snatched the generator back up, concerned that it had been damaged. It looked intact. He placed it back on the table with exaggerated care.

"I'll need that back tomorrow," he said, finger wagging. "I plan to go to another universe tomorrow to finally and definitively prove things to Tracey."

Both of the LaGrues reached for the rift generator, but the one on the left was quicker. He pocketed it with a knowing glance at the other, Ron noted with mild unease.

"Really?" asked Strong. "Where you planning on going?"

"Open up the main screen," Ron motioned to the LaGrues. The LaGrue retrieved the rift generator from his pocket and, after a moment of inspecting the buttons, activated it. The main screen, when not activated for navigation, showed the nearby universe lines like branches on a tree, the nearer ones large and thick, branching off until the fringe ones popped into and out of existence like tiny flashes.

"You see that one?" Ron pointed, "That really fat one, almost as big as ours? The one that has a larger number of little tiny branches, popping in and out like crazy?"

They all peered at the nearby branch, almost like a parallel trunk.

"I scrolled down, which I guess corresponds to 'back in time,' and saw that this other one has run right alongside of ours for a long time. Thousands of years. And sometimes it wraps around our own line, and often even touches it. I'm curious. I want to go see what that one is all about."

"Maybe it is the other side of the mirror, exactly like ours but in reverse," said Strong.

"Maybe," said Ron, with a shrug. "But I intend to find out tomorrow. It will be a good way to try out the orbital pod too."

"I shouldn't be going alone," Ron mused. You want to go?"

"Me?" asked Strong.

"Sure. Unless you'd rather not."

"Uh, sure, I'll go," said Strong, not overly enthusiastic. "But it is just a quick jump to see what it is like over there, then we come right back?"

"Sure," said Ron.

"What if we both go and it turns out that there are no more Pangborn carriers in this universe either?"

"Well that would be bad," Ron said. "But how could that be, if it was in existence before we collapsed the other one?"

"Well, maybe the reason it ended up as a weird mix is because there *wasn't* another universe left, and we had to create a whole new one when we jumped out of the other one."

"Oh come on. There has to be at least one. Somewhere. You just haven't found one yet."

"I know. And I've been looking all over."

"It's a big universe," Ron argued. "And besides, it didn't disappear when I left it before, and you weren't in it then either. So even if it does collapse, maybe it will go back to the one where I was a game programmer and she worked at the Aquarium."

"I don't like this," Tracey protested.

"Really? A few minutes ago, you thought this whole thing was pure insanity. It is just a little jump. One hour. *Five minutes.* You all need proof that this thing works in order to prove my story. What better way?"

Tracey scowled.

A white-uniformed First Mate appeared at the head of the table from the control cabin. "We have arrived at the assembly facility," he announced.

"What was that lurch?" Tracey asked him.

"I don't know ma'am. Sudden wind gust perhaps."

"Ok LaGrues, show us how this thing works," said Ron, watching out the picture window as the flying yacht floated down onto an expanse of concrete that bordered a compound of industrial buildings nestled in a forested valley in the North Cascades. The yacht landed with a barely perceptible jolt, and they filed down the ramp to meet Smithson who was dressed in a black wool pullover and watch cap against the chill air.

"I trust your trip was productive, Mr. Golden," he said with a short bow, falling in beside them as they walked towards the assembly building. It felt good to be out of the drizzle of the Sound area and up in the mountains.

"Indeed it was, my loyal bodyguard," said Ron with an exaggerated flourish. "For we have shown that the twins are not indeed twins but two identical persons, and thus from different universes. And we have also found another way to prove to Tracey and the LaGrues that we are from the alternate universe by way of demonstrating the rift generator."

"That is good, but I could have told you that a long time ago."

"Wait, Smithson," said Tracey, "don't tell me you buy into all this alternate universe stuff too!"

"Ma'am, I do. But only because of my training with the Trident. And with the proper training that you will soon receive, you will be able to remember your partial training and the journeys between the world lines as well. You need to resume your training in dreaming in order to take up your role as a recessive gene holder bodyguard in order to replace me."

Tracey regarded him blankly. "Oooooohhh-kay."

"And to that end," continued Smithson, "I have taken the liberty of setting up an appointment for you to meet with another of our order whom you met while visiting that other universe, a gentleman named Maurice Ring."

"Oh, I remember Maurice!" interrupted Ron. "He was with the Sea Tribes over there." Ron did a classic double take. "Wait a minute, wasn't he burned at the stake? Yes, he was, I watched it happen on TV! How can he be here?"

"How indeed?" asked Smithson.

"Or maybe he is just this universe's version."

They entered the assembly building through a metal door, avoiding the larger roll-up door that was sized to allow large craft to enter and exit. They assembled in a reception area lined with painted portraits of the company's presidents, from Cornish Bob down through Ron's father, who looked little like the jazz bassist he knew and more like a haggard, hawk-eyed industrialist.

"I'll never get over that portrait. That ain't Pop," Ron muttered.

"It was him here," answered Smithson. "Things are not the same in this world that Cornish Bob built. Golden Industries rules the planet."

"Hardly," countered a LaGrue. "There are other corporations giving us a run for our money."

"Please show us the pod," said Ron, changing the subject.

They left the reception area and entered the assembly floor. Groups of workers in yellow coveralls and hardhats stood idly by amid forklifts, scaffolding, robots and other machinery. At their approach, Ron heard a Foreman hiss at the workers, "Get busy, the owner is here!"

The workers exploded into activity, except for an older man with a gray beard who appeared to have trouble standing. He sat back down with a huff.

"All right, old-timer!" proclaimed the foreman, over-loudly for the apparent benefit of the entourage of management. "No slacking off here. Pack your things and get out of here—you're fired."

"Come on, Foreman Powers," pleaded a younger man with angular features. "He's just winded."

Tracey and the LaGrues stopped dead in their tracks and turned their attention on the scene, while Ron almost plowed into their backs. The entire tableau was frozen in silence for long seconds.

"You just got yourself fired too, Jones. For insubordination," growled Foreman Powers.

"Wait, you just fired the guy for sticking up for his coworker?" asked Ron. The foreman's face reddened.

"Good work, Foreman...Powers, is it? Carry on," said Tracey sharply. "Ron, please come with me."

She walked crisply back to the reception area, with Ron in her wake.

"What was that all about?" she said, eyes narrowed.

"I was about to ask you the same question!" Ron retorted.

"You can't go around undermining the staffing decisions of your front-line managers. The Salarymen keep order over the Workers to keep the axles greased and the gears oiled. I don't know how things work in whatever universe you are from, but here we need to stay competitive with other corporations. We pay the lowest wages we can at whatever level we can and get the most work that we can at every level in order to maximize profits. You start undermining the calls of your people, the workforce degrades, the best labor goes elsewhere, the Salarymen go elsewhere, and you are no longer the top company. You have to be ruthless. There are scores of good Workers in line who would kill at the chance to replace that old man and that mouthy little buddy of his."

"Oh yeah, well what happens to them?" said Ron, incredulous.

"Who cares, Ron? They probably join the great unwashed ranks of the Poor, who collect their charity checks and eke out whatever squalid existence their lazy entitled anarchistic asses deserve. Not our concern. Keeping our shareholders, Salarymen and Workers going is. Golden Industries is. Your father would be appalled."

"What happened to you?" asked Ron.

"What happened to *me*?"

Ron bit his lip, mentally vowing to change things.

"And no, you can't change things," Tracey stated. "Things are the way they are and will stay that way."

"We shall see," said Ron. "I am the head of this company after all. Now shall we rejoin the LaGrues and have them show me my new toy?"

They rejoined the group, feigning a carefree air. Ron noted the old man and his young friend exiting the work area, shoulders slumped.

"*Take care of them,*" Ron whispered to Smithson.

—2—

Jeremy Springs ran his index finger along the outside of a smooth, tan thigh, past the barely noticeable string of the bikini bottom on the outside of a perfectly curved hip, then paused in mid-back, torn between advancing north to the knot of the bikini top or retreating south to the territory that beckoned there. He and...Julie? lay on a towel in the sand next to the calmly murmuring surf in the moonlight, under the leaves of a palm tree framed by a million stars, with a pitcher of mango and pineapple margaritas in a bucket of ice nearby.

It sure beat Marine boot camp.

A month prior on training day 62, unknown to Jeremy, Ron Golden, Tracey Springs, and his sister Chris were winging their way to a secret Space Command base under the Denver airport. It was a scant week before graduating from the Marine Corps Recruit Depot in San Diego's Basic training in the First Battalion, Delta Company. His Series Commander had curtly summoned him, with no offer of explanation, to the Commanding General's Office. Such an occurrence, to Jeremy's knowledge, was unheard of.

Upon arrival after a stunned jog across the heat-shimmering concrete parking lot, PFC Springs was escorted into the office of Brigadier General Gregory Thomas. He immediately noted that the General, as he sat behind his desk, chewing on the stub of a cigar, had an expression of repugnance on his face as though he was smoking a turd.

Also standing ill-at-ease nearby was a black man, with sunglasses and earbuds, wearing a nondescript gray suit. Jeremy thought he looked like the quintessential Hollywood central-casting G-Man. The atmosphere was crackling with barely-dissipated tension.

"All right, Private, just who the fuck *are* you?" spat the General.

"Sir?" Jeremy chirped with incomprehension and only just the slightest break in his voice.

"This man has just delivered orders, *from the Commandant himself*, instructing me to pull your ass out of your basic training and remand you to his control. I have been in the Corps for twenty-fucking-seven years, and I have never had this happen or even heard of this happening. *Ever.*"

Jeremy stood stupidly at attention, mind flitting about like a wounded pelican.

"So I repeat. Who the fuck *are* you?"

Jeremy continued his silence, mouth semi-agape.

"I am told that you are the son of someone who has some kind of weird assassins with war-painted faces chasing her. What do you know about that, Private?"

"Sir, NOTHING sir!"

The General furrowed his brow and narrowed his eyes so tightly Jeremy thought his eyeballs would shoot out of his head like watermelon seeds. He noticed that the government agent type was studiously ignoring the entire exchange and had apparently divulged as little as possible—but more than he would have liked—to the General. The General, however, was clearly not used to having his fiefdom invaded by anyone, much less someone from another branch of the military.

"Why would anyone be trying to kill your mother and her significant other, Private?"

"Sir, I have no idea, sir. My mother is a fish scientist, and her boyfriend is...well, he's kind of a boring putz. Sir."

Jeremy realized that this was true and was the main reason he had joined the Marines in the first place. He hadn't wanted to live his whole life in tired obscurity like Ron had. He had wanted to make his mom proud.

Silence settled in and stretched on longer than was necessary or comfortable. But General Thomas eventually convinced himself that even though this turn of events was incomprehensible and outrageous, he could neither control the outcome or would be supplied with any more information. He rose slowly from behind his desk, like an Old Testament patriarch.

"Before I dismiss him," he said gravely, raising his right index finger in an unwavering gesture of warning, "I want him back the *instant* he is done with whatever it is you need him for.

And I must remind you, Private Springs, that you are *very nearly* a United States Marine. And even though you have not yet graduated into my beloved Corps, I expect you to comport yourself at all times with the honor, dignity, and pride of a U.S. Marine. *Is...that...CLEAR?"*

"Sir, YES SIR!"

The general resumed his seat.

"Dismissed," he growled, then busied himself in his paperwork without another thought to the two of them leaving his office.

Jeremy was ushered by the agent into a non-descript white van, taken to an airfield, and loaded into an equally non-descript private jet plane.

On his trip, he was only marginally better at extracting information from the agent than the General was. The agent told him that this name was Johnson. He learned that his mother, older sister Chris, and his mother's boyfriend Ron had been taken somewhere else.

That floored him. Ron had been tapped for some reason by the government. He could not fathom what that was about. While he was not sure what the government would need with a marine biologist, he could at least speculate. But Ron? Ron was a flabby, unemployed game programmer. Unless some covert agency within the United States government had suddenly taken an interest in Pong or Pac Man, he could see no use for him.

He learned that he was in potential danger and was being taken to Andros Island in the Caribbean, along with others similarly at risk. Jeremy had asked him how an island in the Caribbean could be safer than being in the middle of a military base.

The agent assured him that it was.

Jeremy asked in jest whether the painted assassins could beam in like they did in Star Trek, then was surprised when the agent changed the subject.

That struck him as interesting.

After a refueling stop somewhere in Texas, they had continued to the Island, landing late at night.

And the party had commenced.

Jeremy had tried to keep his fitness level up, expecting to be shipped back to San Diego at any time to finish up his basic training. But this had not occurred. His days were spent swimming, sunning, and chasing the numerous young women who had been shipped there as well. There were other young men around, to be sure, but they were hardly the impressive physical specimens that a Marine fresh from boot was.

The only thing keeping him from "getting more tail than a toilet seat in a sorority house" was his sister, who arrived some days later, telling tales of incomprehensible blood tests and aliens and other worlds. She constantly reminded him that while their hosts made sure that there was plenty of alcohol, food, parties, and fun, there were no condoms handed out as part of the package. She was convinced that this was all part of a government plot to breed some kind of recessive genes that she had learned about in a secret base under the Denver Airport. But Jeremy wasn't buying it.

There was, however, something weird going on. The mere fact that a crowd of mostly young adults had been rounded up and deposited on a sandy beach in the Caribbean was unusual enough. But then there were the guys in dark suits, sunglasses and bad haircuts with wires in their ears standing about sweating all over the place. This was indicative of...something. They were not allowed to leave the island, and nobody would say how long they would be there.

Then there was the anti-aircraft battery. It was partially hidden behind some sand dunes and coconut palms, but Jeremy was able to wander around the cluster of three large missiles unchallenged. He had asked one of the "suits" about it and had been told only that the Island was used as a military testing facility when it was not "Club Paradise."

They lived in cabins and had a large common building which was used for dining, dances, parties, and other resort-like activities. Other buildings, farther inland, were off-limits. Jeremy assumed that they were part of the military end of things, including one taller building with a nest of antennas and dishes on the roof.

Four months in, after admiring her from afar, he had met Julie. She was a new friend of his sister Chris, and he had been able to persuade her to listen to him instead of her proclamations of warning and doom. After a three-day whirlwind full-court press, Jeremy had managed to talk her out to the beach in the moonlight, where his hand was now poised in the middle of her goose-fleshed back, torn between trajectories.

It was at that moment when he saw a brief but intense flash of light out at sea, and three seconds later, felt a deep throb in the air, lower than he could hear, but felt in his chest and bones.

It was unlike anything he had ever experienced, and before he could think, he found himself standing on the beach, looking out to sea.

"What was that?" Julie asked, rising to her knees.

Jeremy shushed her, holding up a finger. He scanned the horizon, but could not see anything except a dark blob blotting out a patch of stars, moving slowly towards them, getting larger. It was slower and larger than anything but a zeppelin.

He heard the whine of servo-motors in the sand dune where the anti-aircraft missiles were housed. They were apparently targeting the dark mass.

"Get back to your cabin," Jeremy ordered. She took a few tentative steps, then stopped, watching the massive black shape blotting out the stars get closer.

His mind raced, wondering what to do. He decided to rouse the government agent types. He turned, and one of the missiles fired with a bright lance of blue-hot flame and a deafening roar.

"Well, that should wake them," he mumbled, turning back to watch the missile's flight. The missile traveled halfway to the black shape, then disappeared with a flash. Seconds later, the sound of the explosion reached them, interspersed with the sound of some kind of large caliber gunfire.

"Shit," Jeremy intoned flatly.

Before another missile could fire, the battery behind the dune erupted in an orange fireball, sending shrapnel whooshing over their heads. Jeremy pushed Julie down into the sand, scanning the sky for whatever had destroyed the missile battery. When he found it, his jaw dropped.

It looked like a jet ski, but it was armed with a large caliber gun and small missiles. And it was flying. It streaked overhead, making no noise whatsoever. It was close enough that Jeremy could see the pilot clearly. He was dressed in some sort of skin-tight suit and helmet, and his face was painted with small black lightning bolts on the right cheek. They made eye contact, then he was past, banking sharply to the left, flying inland.

He watched the craft fire at one of the military buildings with a missile. The building with the antennas vanished in the flash of another explosion, the sound reaching them a short time later. Whoever was attacking had just taken out their lines of communication.

"Shit, shit, shit," Jeremy said again, more urgently, crouching on the sand in his bathing suit, wishing he had his M-4 carbine from back at boot camp. He fought the urge to run back towards the cabins and instead scanned the sky for more of the strange craft, unable to get his head around what he had just seen. No such aircraft existed. But there they were, more of the flying jet skis, whipping silently around the island, looking for targets. Occasionally, they fired at a building, and once the government agent and military types began boiling out of buildings, they fired at them as well.

The original large craft now hovered in the sky about a mile offshore, almost visible in the moonlight. It was some kind of spaceship. From it issued four smaller craft, about the size and shape of motor homes. Jeremy knew instantly what they were: troop ships. He watched as they descended to the beach on either side of him in graceful arcs. Large ramps fell open from the front of the craft, and war-paint-wearing men armed with strange-looking guns disgorged from them.

He knew they had no chance. It was over in minutes.

Within an hour, the entire panicky population of the island, including seven surviving government agent types, was herded into two of the landing crafts. Jeremy made sure that he was on the same ship as his sister Chris and their friend Julie. He looked around, stunned, for some idea of who their captors were. The inside of the craft gave no clues: It looked like the inside of any military transport. There was no evidence of the propulsion system, and he could not see any cockpit or weapon stations. There was a row of small windows, and he could just make out the dark beach outside.

There were screams, weeping, shouts for help. The war-painted captors ignored them.

Jeremy and Chris looked at each other with round eyes. She was in her nightshirt.

"Is this a bad time to mention 'I told you so?'" she said, fighting to keep up at least the appearance of not being scared out of her wits.

Jeremy felt an almost-imperceptible sense of motion and knew they had taken off from the island. A glance out the window at the dark ocean below them confirmed this. He heard a burst of radio static from somewhere in the ship, and a flat voice said, "Incoming aircraft, Mach 2. Estimating contact at five minutes. Jump in four."

So they speak English, Jeremy thought. But the military terminology they used was not common to American services. Neither was the face paint, nor the small arms.

Their progress stopped with a metallic clang and a grind of metal against metal. The view outside the porthole was completely obscured by a uniform wall of metal. Jeremy deduced that they had docked to the larger ship.

"Thirty seconds to jump," intoned the radio voice.

"Jeremy, listen to me," Chris whispered fiercely. "I think they are talking about making a jump to another universe. I saw what they called a 'rift' at that base in Denver I told you about. It had a wreck of a ship like this in a yellow desert somewhere on the other side of it. It will make you feel sick."

Jeremy nodded, beyond doubting her anymore.

"Ten seconds to jump," the radio announced.

Jeremy half expected a countdown from that point, but ten seconds later he noticed the soldiers grip their weapons tightly and clinch themselves. He tried to imitate them, but felt an indescribably sickening sensation from his midsection, which quickly passed. Several of the captors vomited.

"Where are we?" he asked Chris. She could only pant with repressed nausea and shrug.

He shouldered his way through the milling captors to one of the portholes and pressed his face against it.

They were in space. Below them was a blue planet, swirled with white clouds.

Shit, he thought again.

"We're in orbit," he called over to Chris. She forced her way to the next porthole.

"That isn't Earth," she announced quietly. Jeremy studied the outlines of the continent below and had to concur. It was nothing he had seen before on any globe or map. They looked at each other, shaking their heads.

There was a burst of static on the speaker, then a voice boomed, "Welcome to Cambria, the home planet of Eiffelia, the

Goddess of the Universe. Soon the airlock will open, and you will proceed into the main ship for processing. You will then be returned to the transports and taken to the planet surface. Resistance to the process will fail and will be punished. Cooperation and compliance will be rewarded."

The airlock door immediately opened with a slight hiss of air equalizing in pressure. The captives moved to the far side of the transport, facing it. Paint-faced armed men cautiously entered and began taking captives out, one at a time. When it was Jeremy's turn, he sized up the soldier quickly, counted the other ones around who were within gun-butt range, and decided to pick his battle for a later time.

He was escorted into what must have been the cargo hold of the ship, where ten small folding tables and chairs had been set up. He was seated at one of them, at the other end of which was a woman in uniform, also with striped make-up, with what looked like a laptop computer. She was attractive, but he noticed that she had a thicker than usual gob of white paint on her upper lip, hiding what he could see were wispy whiskers. The other tables were similarly filled with captives, who were dutifully answering questions. It occurred to Jeremy that they were still in shock and were cooperating out of a sense of familiarity with the procedure, if nothing else.

"Name?" his woman interrogator asked, slender fingers poised over the keyboard.

"Fuck you," Jeremy deadpanned.

"Could you spell that please?" she said, unfazed. Jeremy raised the corner of his mouth with surprise. Maybe they knew the English language, but the apparently didn't know the culture.

"Uh, that would be F-U-K as the first name, and Y-U as the last. My father was Chinese."

"Very well," she continued, tapping the keys. "Age?"

"I'm thirty-seven," he lied.

She looked at him skeptically.

"Look, Madame Moustache, I'm not going to answer your questions," he said, drumming his fingers on the table.

"Mr. Yu, if you do not answer my questions, you will be processed accordingly," the woman said tartly.

"I'm not going to cooperate with you unless I know exactly what is going on here," he said, leaning towards her across the table.

"Next," the woman called to the waiting guards.

Jeremy was taken by the arm and escorted through another airlock into a transport ship. There were six or seven other young men inside.

Time passed. Jeremy had no idea how long. He was hungry, thirsty, and tired.

Soldiers came and forcibly took blood samples from all of them, then left. Jeremy decided to bide his time and not fight them. More time passed and he slept.

A loud clanging noise woke him with a start. He was sitting with his back to the cold bulkhead, and his butt was numb.

Must have fallen asleep, he thought. He noticed that the airlock door had closed. He jumped to his feet and crossed rapidly to a window. They were falling away from the main ship.

He wheeled about and saw only the same seven young men in pajamas and shorts, guarded by two stripe-faced soldiers. Chris was not among them.

His stomach fell and a lump formed in his throat.

I am going to kill each and every one of you motherfuckers, he thought, staring directly at one of the soldiers. But it did not make him feel any better.

Red light began flickering across the windows then intensified in brightness. Jeremy postulated that they were entering the planet's atmosphere. He stared out of a window, trying to see where they were going. For a while, all he could see was a uniform fiery red. They slowed, and the friction of entering the atmosphere lessened into a high-altitude flight.

They were flying over an ocean. Far away on the horizon, but growing closer, was a dark smudge of a landmass. It resolved into a narrow stretch of land between the sea and a cliff. At first, the cliff looked small, but as they neared the coast, the scale became clearer. It was a *tall* cliff, very sheer and rocky.

They dropped further in altitude and slowed. The land appeared to be only a few miles wide and was liberally coated in trees and tropical vegetation. Jeremy could not see any buildings or other structures.

The landing craft settled soundlessly on the wide, white sand beach. It occurred to Jeremy that, only a short time before, they had been plucked off a similar-looking beach, and he had no idea whatsoever how far away that beach was or even if it was in the same universe.

The door ramp descended and nestled into the sand with a soft "whump."

Jeremy glanced at the guards, who motioned them towards the beach. He considered attacking them at that point but was unsure of what that would gain him unless he could somehow commandeer the ship.

The eight young men shuffled uncertainly out of the ship, down the ramp, and onto the sand. Their guards stayed on the ship. They heard the ramp rise behind them. Jeremy turned in time to see the ship lift from the sand and float away, slowly at first, then at great speed.

At least they didn't shoot us in the back.

It was hot. The sand burned his bare feet. The surf murmured. The eight of them stood in stunned silence, wondering what to do next.

Jeremy scanned the tree line a hundred yards away and saw movement. He pointed, and the others in his group followed his gaze.

Out of the trees and tropical brush ran a group of five men. They were lean and wiry, darkly tanned, dressed in rags, with long hair and beards. They came straight at them and stopped a short distance away. Jeremy studied them. They looked almost like cave men.

"Got any food?" One of them panted.

Jeremy shook his head. The wild men probed them carefully with their eyes, looking for anything to eat that they might be hiding, but the eight of them fresh from the transport were dressed only in pajamas or shorts.

"Where are we?" asked one of the former captives.

The head wild-man ignored him, smiling. He glanced back over his shoulder at the tree line.

"You guys don't have long until they get here," he said.

"Until who gets here?" asked Jeremy.

The cave man smiled with an evil nod.

"Just run, boys. As long as you keep moving, they won't catch you."

With a last smirk, the whole hairy group of them trotted off down the beach.

The new arrivals stood uncertainly, looking nervously towards the trees. When they saw what crawled out of the forest, they turned as one and ran too.

—3—

"So we're going to use the orbital pod thing, right?" asked Jack Strong.

"I think that would be safer. I mean, if we end up on land, no biggie. But if we end up in space or in an ocean or something, or in the middle of a mountain, it would be better to have some kind of skin of pressurized metal and glass around us at least," answered Ron, motioning to the door.

The orbital pod was about the size of a Winnebago. It had similar sleeping quarters, a kitchenette, a bathroom, storage lockers, and a bank of communication and navigation controls. The LaGrue twins had done their best to make the craft as stealthy as possible, with shielding and black-painted composite materials. It was capable of being operated in zero gravity, or up to 300 meters underwater.

"I bet this thing cost a pretty penny," Strong said, cautiously entering through the hatch. Are we missing something?" They sat for a moment staring at each other.

"Oh, the rift generator! Won't be going far without that."

The LaGrues appeared and reached into the craft with the generator. Ron caught a barely perceptible look that passed between the two twins before they left but could not make anything from it. He checked the device, saw that it was intact. He placed the instrument into a special receptacle designed for it, and the systems and display screens powered up.

"So...what do we do?" asked Strong.

"I just enter the coordinates for the alternate universe branch thusly," Ron said, tapping the keyboard at the console. "Press the button and voila! New universe."

"Wait..." Jack said, while Ron's finger hovered over an oversized red button. "We are forgetting something else."

"What now?" Ron asked impatiently.

"We haven't closed the door."

"Holy shit," Ron said. "If we ended up in space that would have ruined our day."

Strong gave him a "You idiot, you are rushing things without adequately preparing for crazy eventualities" kind of a look, and Ron unbuckled himself from his padded chair and went back to the door.

Tracey was waiting for him just outside.

Shit, he thought.

She looked at him with intensity. He waited for her to speak.

"You can't go. We have an appointment with that friend of yours who burned at the stake later this morning."

"I'll be back by then."

"Ron. I *really think you should not go*."

Something in her tone gave him pause.

"I'll be back in five minutes. *Five minutes*, babe. It must be safe: I'm using the exact same jump setting that Cornish Bob used in the past, and he made it back."

He closed the door, sealed it properly for vacuum like the LaGrues had taught him, then strapped back into his seat.

"I dunno, man, she sounded like she was serious. You don't listen to her enough," Strong said.

Ron rolled his eyes, as though asking whether Jack Strong was a real man or a whipped mouse. But between the weird look from the LaGrues and now Tracey's earnestness, something gave him pause.

Nah.

"All right, dude," Strong shrugged. "But if we die, I'm holding you responsible."

"We won't die," Ron said. "I have a good feeling about this. And if we want to take our time, we can set the return to five minutes from now, and I won't even break my promise to Tracey. Hell, we could use a vacation."

He pushed the jump button.

Neither of them felt the nausea that others did upon jumping, as they were both double recessives. They leaned forward to look out of the window to see where they had ended up.

They saw a grassy area, covered with patches of snow. Beyond that was a rock wall.

"So far so good," said Ron. He checked the consoles like the twins had taught him.

"Gravity 1.0, nitrogen oxygen atmosphere...looks ok. So unless we have some kind of bugs to worry about, we are cool to go explore."

"So we just get out? Just like that? What if there *are* weird viruses and all?"

"Five minutes, Jack. Let's just look around a *little*."

"You go first," Strong said, motioning to the door.

Ron unsealed it, and it swung free to let in a fresh, green smell from the grasses and snow.

Ron stepped out onto the ground.

"That's one small step for a man...one...giant leap for Golden Industries," Strong called from the interior. Strong joined him outside.

The pod rested in a field on the side of a mountainside. It was a gentle slope. The patches of snow grew larger the higher up the mountain they looked, until at higher elevations, the snow was everywhere. They could not see the summit.

Farther down, the grasses grew taller into sparse bushes, and farther downhill yet they could see the green of treetops. The sound of a stream downhill reached them.

"Aha, we must get a water sample for the LaGrues," Ron said, starting downhill.

"Wait...what about the whole five minutes thing?" Strong protested.

"That's all it will take—it isn't that far," Ron said, starting downhill.

Something about the scenery, the crisp air, and the sun made Strong almost intoxicated. He could tell Ron was flushed and invigorated too.

They walked.

Ron felt actually drunk but knew he hadn't been drinking.

They had walked for what seemed longer than five minutes, but Strong had ceased to care.

"I love to go, a wandering..." Ron started singing.

"Along the mountain track..." Strong joined in, with exaggerated gusto.

"And as I go, I *love* to sing, *my knapsack on my back!*"

"Val-de-RI, val-de RA, val-der-RI, val-der-A-HA-HA...." Their song tailed off into silence as they saw three small red cones moving through the tall grasses ahead of them.

The two men stopped and gripped each other's arms to steady themselves, wondering what to do.

"What the hell are those?" Ron whispered over-loudly.

"Shhh!" Strong shushed, finger against lips.

The red cones stopped, then advanced more slowly. Ron and Strong barely heard little voices.

Ron was torn between running for the ship and staying to see what the red cones were. Curiosity won out.

Presently, the red cones emerged from the tall grass, and it became clear that they were the tops of red conical hats, worn by rotund little men with gaily-colored clothes and fluffy white beards.

"Holy crap, they're friggin' *lawn gnomes*!" Strong pointed and erupted in laughter.

"Shut up, Jack." Ron said quietly, suddenly possessed with an ominous mood. Just as suddenly, though, the mood lifted and was replaced by a mixture of confusion, portent, and giddiness.

The two groups regarded each other silently for a space.

"And who be ye two?" asked one of the gnomes with a reedy, British-accented voice.

"I'm Ron and this is Jack."

The gnomes nodded and glanced at each other knowingly. Ron thought he detected a vast intelligence in their eyes.

"Vat are you doing here, Ron and Jack?" asked one of the other gnomes, this one with a German accent.

'Uh, just visiting?" said Ron.

"Just visiting, he says," chimed in the third gnome, this one with a New Jersey accent.

"Dat's vat dey all say," said German gnome.

"Until they show their true colors by trying to steal our gold," said English gnome.

"I thought that was elves who had the gold," said Ron quietly.

"You're thinking of Leprechauns," said Jack.

"Oh, right. Wait, I thought they were worried about getting their Lucky Charms stolen, not gold?" Ron did his best to stifle a laugh, but was barely able to contain it. The entire situation was beyond ridiculous.

"They think we're funny," said New Jersey gnome.

"No, sorry, not funny. Just this whole place is making me feel weird. What is this place, anyway?"

"Yes, dat's vat it is. Anyway," said German gnome.

"Or Anywhere," said English.

"Or Any Youngman," said New Jersey, and all three of them laughed.

"Any fool vill tell you that Anybody with Any sense von't be doing you Any favors by Any means in Any way, shape or form by giving you Any lip," deadpanned German.

"At Any rate, is there Any truth to the rumor that you two buffoons aren't Any good at figuring Anything out?" asked English.

"I'm not figuring out how there are living, breathing lawn gnomes here. What are the odds that you evolved in this universe exactly like the porcelain ones in our world look?" asked Jack.

"Not to pull Any punches, we're breathing all right," said New Jersey, "but we aren't living. Not how you know it, in Any event. We're Made, not Begotten like you mooks, by Any stretch."

Ron and Strong glanced at each other, then stared at the gnomes stupidly.

"What do you mean? Made? Not Begotten?"

"You haven't Any idea what we're talking about?" asked English.

"No idea," said Ron. "Not by any stretch of the imagination."

The gnomes burst out laughing.

"Good one!" said German gnome. "Any vay you slice it!"

Ron's head was spinning. *Enny...Enny...Enny...*

"I'm tired of this game," said New Jersey. "Let's not take it Any further...."

The gnomes burst out laughing anew. They watched Ron and Strong carefully.

"Look at them, lads! They're going to Any lengths not to say Anything with Any in it!"

"I'm not going to say it. You won't get any such satisfaction from me," Jack said.

The gnomes fell on the ground laughing.

"Did I say...? Oh shit. Ron, let's get back to the ship. I can't take any more of this."

More laughter, pounding on the ground with tears.

"Go ahead, it won't bother us....Any!" English gnome managed between gasps.

Ron thought very carefully about what he was going to say next and made sure that there was no trace of the word "any" in it.

"Thank you for your company," he said deliberately, "but we must get back to our world now."

The gnomes groaned with disappointment that Ron had killed the streak.

"You can't go yet; you haven't seen the Sacred Mountain. Or the Sacred Grass Fields. Or the Sacred Forest, or our Holy Hovels. Or the most revered of all, the Sacred Gardens of Gnome," said German.

"Sorry, but we were only popping over here for a short time to see what it was all about. We have to leave now."

"Oh, you *can't* leave," said New Jersey, his eyes growing round with enthusiasm. "Not without joining the Sacred Elf Dance. Or the Sacred Elf Orgy. Or seeing the Unicorns, or the Trolls. Or the Sacred Rainbow Waterfall!"

"We're really sorry, but we *have* to go," said Jack.

"No, *we're* really sorry, but you *can't* go."

"And why is that?" Ron asked, growing irritated.

"Because we have the wee gold ball," the English gnome said, and held up the small gold rift generator that had been installed in the ship's navigation panel.

Ice water flooded Ron's veins.

"You need to give that back," he said, suddenly stone sober.

"If you can catch us," laughed the German gnome. The three gnomes suddenly grabbed their red hats and broke into a full run downhill for the forest.

Ron and Strong pelted after them.

*****

Tracey lifted up the paper, which was wrapped in a plastic bag with two rubber bands. She held it up for Ron to see from the picture window, informing him that the Times at least thought it was going to rain.

But Ron wasn't there in the picture window like he always was.

"That's odd," she thought, wondering what was drawing him away from their morning ritual.

Probably too much coffee requiring an emergency trip to the bathroom. She hoped he would actually do something to find a job that day, instead of sit around in his bathrobe and watch TV or play that stupid video game again.

She drove her bug the usual route to the Seattle Aquarium, noting unusually heavy traffic on Aurora as it crossed the ship canal.

Once at her desk, she booted her computer up and adjusted the model of the blue ring octopus while the home screen loaded. She checked her calendar and saw that under the 9:00 time slot there was a single name listed: Maurice.

"Claire," she called to her assistant, "who is the 'Maurice' I have at nine?"

"Dunno," her assistant called from the next office. "You've had that on the calendar for a while. He's actually waiting downstairs in the lobby; he came early."

Tracey arched her eyebrows. She had no memory of setting the appointment or who this guy was or what he wanted.

"Did he say what he wants?"

"You set the appointment. I have no idea."

"Well, show him in," Tracey said, deciding to fish around tactfully until she could remember who the man was, hopefully without embarrassing herself.

Maurice was shown in and took a seat in a chair across from Tracey's desk. Maurice turned out to be a black man with long hair, dressed in a fine suit.

"Thank you for seeing me," he said warmly, then smiled and regarded her in silence for an uncomfortably long pause.

"Mr. ...Maurice, I am at a loss. Is Maurice your last name?" she stumbled.

"Oh, no, it is my first name. And I apologize—when we set this appointment originally things were quite different. You probably have no idea who I am, aside from the faintest sense of familiarity, maybe a feeling in the back of your mind that we might have met somewhere else but you can't remember."

Tracey shrugged. "Actually, no. I have no memory of making the appointment or who you are. I'm sorry."

"Ah," Maurice said, templing his fingers. "It is indeed a whole new world."

"What do you mean?" she asked.

"Ms. Springs, I'm going to tell you something. And you are going to have a hard time believing it, but I'm going to ask you the courtesy of hearing me out."

"Ok," she agreed. "I'm intrigued."

Maurice pursed his lips, nodded slightly, looking for where to begin.

"This morning, you and your husband Ron were the richest people on the planet, but when he and his friend Jack Strong used his rift generator to jump to another universe, it caused the universal bubble that had been artificially created by his ancestor by jumping back to the nineteenth century to collapse because he and Jack Strong were the last double recessives in that universe. When they left, the universe collapsed into this one, which was the one that you and he had previously left to travel over to another universe, where you met with the Sea Tribes and where I was burned at the stake. Now your husband and Jack Strong are trapped in Hell, and you are going to need to continue your training to rescue them."

Tracey nodded, nonplussed.

"Is that it?" she asked.

"Not even remotely," confessed Maurice feebly.

"Well, Maurice with no last name, that is all very interesting, but first of all, Ron and I are not married, and I have no idea who Jack Strong is, and the rest of what you said really makes no sense whatsoever. But what do you mean Ron is trapped somewhere?"

"I'm afraid that the world that he and Jack Strong jumped to is not really another universe bubble like others, but a companion one to this universe that is caused by the creative process of quantum collapsing from the collective consciousness of humanity, brought about by divine fiat. Some call it Faerie, some call it Hell. It is populated by all manner of beings made up by humanity, as well as an alternate population of humanity with other ground rules. They are trapped there."

Tracey's eyes narrowed. She remembered back to the empty window that morning. Had this lunatic done something to him? She picked up the phone on her desk and dialed her house. There was no answer. She hung up and dialed Ron's cellphone. His voice mail picked up. She felt a pang of worry, and mentally convinced herself that he had probably forgotten to pay the cellphone bill again.

"Have you kidnapped Ron?" she asked sharply.

"Oh no. But you will find that he is not at home anymore. You will have to join me to train to go to that world and rescue them."

"Mr. Maurice, I think it's time for you to leave. But just in case I need to find you, where can I reach you?"

"I will have to find you," he said enigmatically, standing.

"My, how hackneyed-sounding. Really, do you have an address or a telephone number?"

"Truthfully, no to both. But I will promise to be back in three days, and maybe by then you will be ready to join me to begin your training. Actually, to *resume* your training."

Tracey was not sure what else to say but was glad the mentally-ill person was leaving her office.

"Well, good day, sir," she managed as he left with an odd little bow.

Tracey called Claire in to her office.

"Claire, if that guy ever comes back, call security. He was telling me some weird stuff about how Ron and some guy I've never heard of are trapped in Hell."

"You want me to call the cops?" her assistant asked.

Tracey considered it.

"No, what would I tell them? Ron isn't exactly missing yet. He's probably out looking for work," she said, not really believing it.

This is going to be a long day, she thought.

It was.

When she finally got home after fighting her way through the drizzle-exacerbated rush hour traffic, Ron was not at home, even though his car was. There were no dishes from him in the sink. In a near panic, she dialed his cellphone again. She heard it ringing in the bedroom and ran to discover it on the bed, along with his keys and wallet. His bathrobe was hanging on the hook on the wall behind the door. It was as though he had simply vanished.

Shit.

She picked up the telephone to call the police, but vacillated. She knew that, at least on TV, they told people they couldn't start considering him missing until he had been gone twenty-four hours, but she wanted to do something.

She called anyway and was indeed told by the dull-sounding policeman that she would have to wait twenty-four hours from when he was last seen. She told him about the long-haired black man in the suit who had visited her that morning, telling her that Ron had been trapped in what he had described as Hell. The policeman seemed more interested, but still they could do nothing. She hung up in despair.

She did not sleep all that night, expecting every slight noise to be Ron returning from...wherever he had gone. All sorts of thoughts ran through her head as she lay in the bed, the lights still on. Had he killed himself? He had been depressed about not having a job, feeling useless and directionless. But there was no note, and Ron was not one to do something like that. Was he out partying with friends at a strip club or something? She knew that wasn't like him either.

It must be that Maurice guy, kidnapping him then telling her about it so...so what? He could convince her to go resume training for something? Why not a demand for ransom?

Morning came and she called the police again. They sent around a car with two polite officers who took down what information they could and said that they would begin the process of looking for him.

She decided to stay home from work, to see if Ron would come waltzing in which he would probably do at any moment.

He did not.

Nor did he appear on the second day. The police had no leads, aside from her description of Maurice. They could not find either Ron or Maurice. Her despair grew. She remembered that Maurice had told her that he would come back to see her on the third day. She called the police detective who had been assigned the case, a detective Ramsey. They planned an ambush instead of going public with a news story about a missing person.

On the third day, she went to work, while the police lingered about behind the scenes. At precisely nine o'clock, Claire called her to inform her that Mr. Maurice had come to see her.

"Please tell him to come in," she instructed Claire.

Maurice came and sat in the same chair.

"Before the police come and take me," he said, "I want to tell you that they will not be able to hold me, and I will come visit you at your home tonight. And I will ask you again to join me to resume your training."

Detective Ramsay and three uniformed Seattle Policemen stormed the office, guns drawn, and threw Maurice to the floor of her office, cuffing him. The three officers took him away, with a last knowing glance over his shoulder at her. Ramsay remained behind.

She was shaking.

"We'll question him," the detective said, "and he'll probably let something slip. Crazy people tend to do that. But if he doesn't, we can only hold him so long before we have to charge him with something. And right now, we don't have any evidence of anything to charge him with. We'll keep you posted."

The rest of the day crawled by, every phone call possibly the one informing her that Maurice had cracked and told the interrogators where the pit that Ron was buried in was located. Finally, at almost four o'clock, it was detective Ramsay on the line.

"He didn't tell us anything. Anything we believed, anyway."

Tracey placed her fist against her temple and squeezed her eyes shut.

"He said he would get loose and visit me at my house tonight," she said after a long sigh. "Could you have an officer stay with me?"

"Ma'am, that will be unnecessary. This guy is going to be the guest of King County for a while. Seventy-two hours, at least."

When she got home later, it was deep into dusk. The house was dark. She unlocked the mailbox and glanced at the letters in the light of the porch while she fished in her purse for her keys. Mostly bills, but one important-looking letter from the Department of the Navy.

She unlocked the door, threw her keys on the foyer table. She turned on the light, and her heart almost stopped. Maurice was sitting at the dining room table.

"Don't be afraid," he said.

Strangely, she wasn't. Her primal danger warning bells were not ringing.

"I thought you were in jail," she said, trying to be nonchalant, taking off her scarf and laying it on the couch.

"I was," he said. "But dying has its advantages. Optional corporealness being one of them."

"You are a ghost?" she asked, disbelieving, and sat at the table with him. She tossed the mail on the table next to her.

He rapped on the table with his knuckles. "When I need to be."

"So if I called down to the jail, you would be there or be gone?"

"Why don't you call and find out?"

She pulled out her cellphone, but it rang before she could start figuring out how to call the jail. She answered it.

"Ms. Springs, this is Detective Ramsay. I have some bad news. This is really embarrassing, but your kidnapper has somehow managed to escape. I'm going to send some officers by right away, since he said he was going to go to your house. You are at your house, aren't you?"

"Actually, I'm still driving there. I should be there in twenty minutes," she found herself lying.

"We'll have a car there in fifteen," Detective Ramsay said.

"Thank you, Detective," she said, hanging up. "That gives you *ten*," she said to Maurice. "Convince me."

Maurice nodded, still sitting at the table. He looked tired.

"I want you to keep an open mind here, but this is going to be very, very hard for you to accept. I'm going to ask simply that you trust me. I told you earlier what went on that morning three days ago. Your...husband, who here is not your husband, has a rare gene that keeps universes from collapsing when they otherwise would. His friend Jack Strong also had it. When they left to go explore what they thought was an alternative universe, it left this universe with no more double recessives. There is an evil being, who you already had conflict with in another universe, who had done a thorough job of killing off all the other double recessives. So when Ron and Jack left, it collapsed the universe back into what it was before you both left to go to the universe I was originally from. So here you are, with no Ron because he ran into some...entities, for lack of a better term, over there who took his 'rift generator,' a small machine that allows jumps between universes."

He paused to gauge her reaction. She had none, and continued to sit still.

"So tell me, since I'm still not sure how all this shook out a few days ago. Does Ron have any children?"

"No," she said guardedly, suddenly even more suspicious. "But I do."

"I was afraid of that," Maurice frowned. "They are probably missing too, aren't they?"

Tracey picked up her phone again and dialed Chris' cell number.

"Hello?" answered a sleepy girl's voice. But it was not Chris' voice.

"Who is this?" Tracey snapped.

"This is Tanya," the girl said.

"May I speak to Chris?" Tracey asked, trying to sound calm.

"She's not here right now," said the girl. "I'm her roommate. Who is this?"

"I'm her mom. Where is she, and why isn't she carrying her phone?"

"I don't know. I haven't seen her for a few days. She may be with her boyfriend. Can I take a message for her in case I see her tomorrow?"

Tracey's insides locked with unease.

"Sure, tell her that she needs to call her mom *right away.*"

Then she remembered the letter from the military. She snatched it up, fear giving way to anger. Phrases jumped out from the letter: *Unauthorized Absence...Article 86(3) of the Uniform Code of Military Justice..."Absentee" pursuant to MCO 5800.10...Surrender to Military Authority as soon as possible....*

"All right, you bastard. How can you kidnap *all three of them?*"

He looked at her with helpless pity.

"You couldn't. Not all three."

He let her sit for a while in silence.

"So now you have to do something. You can help them. It is not all bad news."

"Talk to me. And you better be quick, the cops are on the way."

"You went over to that other universe with Ron and several other people. You actually stayed with me and a friend for a while, before I was captured and killed. You escaped her and lived with the Sea Tribes for a while and started your training, unbeknownst to you, with one of our number. You have met some of us: Silas Bell, Mr. Stone, Ms. Lake—they are the Mods. You also met some others of us, like me and Smithson: We are members of the Trident, who work with them."

Her memory stirred, squirmed like a snake under bed sheets. "I escaped from who? Who killed you?"

"Her name is Eiffelia."

Tracey's skin crawled at the name. Something wordless stirred in her memory.

"Ah, I see you start to remember. You will remember more, after you begin the next phase of your training in the Trident."

"The Trident? Kind of gummy sounding," she said.

"Gummy it may sound, but not many are called to serve in this way, and even fewer are chosen." he said.

"What do I have to do to get Ron and my kids back?"

"Ron first; kids are another matter. His path leads to rescuing them from her, with your help and protection."

"Ok, fine. What do I have to do?" she repeated curtly.

"You will wait, at first. I know you are impatient, but you will have to wait until you have a dream that takes you to Andrew Morrow's Scrytorium."

"His what?"

"His Scrytorium. Dream Andrew Morrow, and you will find the way."

"Who is that?"

"I'm out of time," Maurice said, glancing out the picture window at the police car pulling up in the driveway. He stood, walked to the back door, and paused.

"One thing I forgot to mention that you might have forgotten but needs reminding," he said hurriedly. "Andrew Morrow is one of the Mods, and as such he is not a human being. Just sayin'."

He wrapped his suit coat around him a bit more tightly, and with a glance over his shoulder at her with a ghostly half smile, vanished into the night like smoke.

—4—

"*Fuk Yu indeed,*" thought Elanor 32 as the brash young captive was led away to the Food Shuttle. Those captives would be taken to the edge of Cambria's main continent if they were lucky. On some days, on a schedule beyond Elanor's knowledge, the captives would simply be dropped into the ocean to feed Eiffelia's prehistoric sharks. At least on the beaches, they had a chance against her giant scorpions.

"Next," she called.

A young woman with long, brown hair was led in by the security force soldier. She had big, brown eyes, but they were not as glassy and terrified as the others she had processed before. Instead, she looked earnest and quiet.

"Name?" she asked reflexively.

"Chris Springs. And I want to be taken to wherever my brother was taken."

Elanor kept her eyes on her computer screen, avoiding the uncomfortable gaze of the captive girl."

"What is his name?" Elanor asked.

"Jeremy Springs."

Elanor looked at the intake master list on another screen.

"We have no Jeremy Springs."

"He must be on there—he was taken out before me," the girl pleaded.

Elanor pursed her lips.

"We do have a young gentleman who has a faint family resemblance to you by the name of 'Fuk Yu' who came through a short time ago," she said wryly.

"That's him," said the girl immediately, with the flash of a frustrated smile. "I want to be sent wherever he goes."

Elanor's finger hovered over the keyboard. Unbidden, and from an unknown place in her mind, she made a fateful decision that could endanger her life. The choice was made instantly, and she knew that once made, it could not be undone if the girl before her made the slightest hesitation or mistake. But she knew she must make it, in spite of the danger to herself and the other six members of her secret cell.

"No," she said quietly, still looking at the keyboard as though she were working. "You do *not* want to go where he goes. You must listen very carefully to what I am going to tell you, and you must trust me or we both are going to die. Do you understand?"

The girl nodded, her brown eyes widening slightly.

Elanor took a deep breath.

"You are here to be processed. I am one of the people whose job it is to process new people. This planet is the home world of Eiffelia, the Goddess. She looks like the spirit of a woman, but she isn't really. She is a giant sponge, as big as the whole ocean of this world. She has been growing for millions of years here. Human beings were brought here by her to serve her, and we do, but mostly only because we are given drugs to make us stupid and compliant. Me and a few friends have managed to avoid taking the drugs, and we meet in secret to help each other and...well, you will learn later what else. But for now, I have to keep you from being processed in the wrong line. Most of the people brought to this world are brought here for one reason: food. The rest are just slaves. For this shipment, she will try to breed you for your special genes. That is why they took the blood from you: to test you for them. If you have the genes, you will be bred, if you don't, you will be food. We have to be very careful, very skillful and secret, to keep any of that from happening. I'm risking my life to help you."

She paused to see what affect her words were having on the new girl. She was sitting quietly, trying to take it all in.

"So I am going to enter your name in the system as Carla 23. I am going to list your blood test as 'negative.' I am going to assign you to a job of 'Pharmaceutical Technician.' When you get down to the planet surface and see the others being herded into a line for assignments, do not get in the line. Go to the second line, the one that is handing out the little electronic devices. When they tell you to put your thumb on the thumb pad, do it in such a way that the middle of your thumb does not come in contact with the hole in the middle: That is where a little needle would pop out and inject you with the drug. Don't let it stick you, but do whatever you have to do to make them think you did! Then walk towards the nearest large double doors and tell any security guard that you have already been assigned.

Show them the form that I will print out for you. Are you with me so far?"

The brown haired girl nodded, nervously.

"You can't be afraid. You have to act like all the other people around you: dull, happy, and stupid. Can you do that?"

The girl nodded.

"Good. Then you have to follow the directions on your form to your living room. It may be difficult for you, since you are probably not used to the architecture. But I don't have time to explain that to you. Then at seven o'clock, you have to be at the other address I am going to print out for you, on a different little paper. That is where our group will meet you and give you more instructions and help. If you are caught, do not give them that address. Eat it if you have to. Do you understand, Carla 23?"

The girl nodded once again.

"Good. Because if you fail, we both die, along with my friends."

Elanor printed out a form and handed it to the girl, along with a smaller piece of paper with her cell's address.

"Thank you," the girl whispered, and went to join the others who had been processed in the shuttle.

"Next," Elanor called to the guards, and they brought another of the captives to her for processing. She resisted the urge to do the same thing for this young man. Out of the hundreds, the thousands that she had processed in this way, this was the only time she had risked herself for one.

What have I done? She began casting about for reasons to give her cell members, but none would come.

She busied herself processing the rest of the new captives, then joined the other workers on the shuttle back to Cambria's main human city, the City of God.

One of her coworkers, a young man who Elanor imagined had designs on her, greeted her in the usual drug-induced haze.

"Hello Elanor 32!" he said brightly.

"I feel 'ya, Jurgen 18!" she replied cheerfully.

"Eiffelia too!" he replied. "You wanna come over and watch TV with me tonight? Super Jumbo Penises is on!"

"No thanks, Jurgen, I'm busy meeting with someone else," she said. He looked mildly disappointed, but seconds later his eyes drifted off into the drug-induced haze again.

The shuttle undocked from the big Cruiser and dropped back into the planet's atmosphere. After the fiery reentry, the antigrav engines kicked in, and they glided into one of the large spherical landing bays of the city.

Walking into the City of God, it occurred to Elanor that she should have given the new girl more instructions for navigating there. It was not constructed with human beings in mind, apparently, but through the mind of a sponge. It was as though an enormous slag of melted plastic had been suddenly cooled, with large and small gas bubbles freezing into roughly spherical chambers, which were then connected with a warren of roundish tubes of various sizes. After she learned the truth about Eiffelia, she recognized it for what it was: a larger-scaled representation of the structure of a sponge.

Elanor checked her PC for the time and realized she would have to hurry to make it to the weekly meeting of her cell. She would have to do the best she could to prepare them for the newly invited member and risk their wrath.

She made her way through the warren of tunnels as quickly as she could without appearing to hurry. When she neared the turnoff to their meeting room, she made sure that nobody was in the curving tunnel to see her, then ducked suddenly down the side passage to the meeting room. The standing plan was that if anyone stumbled upon the meetings, they would act as though it was a prayer group.

Rosa 40 was already there, huddled in the back of the oval shaped chamber with protrusions from the wall that they used as seats. She was a pleasant and handsome woman who worked as a medical technician.

Elanor took a seat opposite her without saying a word, and they waited for the others.

Cain 10 was the next to arrive. He was an angular man with hollow eyes, a former soldier, who now worked with explosives at the weapons manufacturing plant. He took another seat and nodded to them both in greeting.

Elanor wondered when Chris Springs would show up and what she would say to them all, especially Anton 36, the self-styled leader of the group.

Valentina 69 arrived next. She was a beautiful blonde woman, their celebrity, who had her own porn show. They hoped that once the revolution was launched, she could use her ties in the media to transmit the message to the newly freed populace.

Anton came shortly thereafter and glanced around quickly.

"It looks like we're all here," he said, sitting down with a loud exhalation. "Let's get started."

"Actually, we're not all here," Elanor said quietly. "I just recruited someone else."

There was shocked silence.

"What do you mean, you recruited someone else?" hissed Anton. "Who said you could do that?"

"Nobody said I could," Elanor retorted. "And nobody said I couldn't either. You are always saying how we have no official leaders; nobody is higher ranked than anyone else around here. I had an opportunity and made a call."

They all looked at her with suspicion, shock, and anger. She met their gazes. Even though Anton said repeatedly that he was not the official leader, it was unspoken that he was.

"Who is it?" asked Cain.

"A girl. Fresh from the off-world shuttle. I caught her before she could be drugged up with Xylol, so there won't be any problems like we had with detoxing. And there's no way she could be a spy. We need a backup plan to our current one, or maybe an extra wrinkle to it. I assigned her to work as a Pharmacy Tech right at the Xylol plant."

Elanor watched as this information worked through the minds of her group.

It was then that Chris Springs appeared in the doorway, looking scared and lost.

"Sit down, Carla 23," said Elanor.

"It's Chris, really," she said feebly.

"Not anymore," said Anton, once again trying to regain the mantle of leadership. "Your name is now Carla 23. Mine is Anton 36. I'm a Shuttle Pilot. This is Valentina 69, Rosa 40, and Cain 10. We call ourselves the Virii. We are little viruses living in the body of Eiffelia, without her knowledge, and hope to make her very sick someday. And you are going to help us."

"Do you understand the danger we are all in?" asked Rosa quietly from the corner.

"I looked and listened to people on the way here," answered Chris. "They all seem dead, drugged, empty."

"Exactly," said Valentina. "We were lucky enough to have some natural resistance to the drug that Eiffelia uses to control us. One of us, Anton, managed to stop taking it but acted like he still was. He was able to get into the computers and find us. Because we had more natural resistance, he looked for people who were getting massive doses to keep us in the same state as others. With me, he just watched my show and could tell. One by one, he was able to help us by asking us to join his prayer group, then showing us how to avoid the thumb sticks where the drug is administered. Now we just act like we're drugged, like everyone else."

"Now we're trying to free all of us from her drugs," added Anton. "We are a planet full of slaves who don't even know they are."

"If we are discovered, we'll be killed," added Rosa. That was enough for Chris.

"Ok, look," she said, holding up her palms. "I wish you the best and all, but this is not my fight. I'm sure you guys are in a worthy crusade and all, but I'm sorry, I just want to find my brother and go home."

The conspirators glanced between themselves, and it occurred to Elanor that they were considering killing the newcomer to prevent her revealing them.

"Carla....*Chris*, wait," she said. "Maybe we can help each other. There is no way you can find your brother on your own. I work in personnel assignments. I might be able to find him. You help us, we help you."

Chris' eyes narrowed. She considered her options.

"What is the plan?" she asked.

"That's just it," said Anton, "we haven't settled on a final version yet."

"That's because every scenario we have come up with, some combination of Anton flying a shuttle with explosives stolen by Cain into the orbiting drug factory, involves us dying at the end," said Valentina with pursed lips.

"We've never had anyone on the inside, actually *in* the manufacturing facility, until now," Elanor said excitedly. "She can destroy the process from the inside. Sabotage. Maybe without explosives, even, so the process can be rendered harmless while making it look like a manufacturing failure. Then we get you out of there on Anton's shuttle, while the harmless drug gets shipped out and fails to drug the populace. Valentina then gets the word out on the TV."

"And you find my brother and get us back to our home planet," nodded Chris. "I guess we have a deal then."

"So for now," Elanor continued, "you just get started on your new job and learn all you can about it. I'll get on the computers and try to find your brother. The rest of us stand by and keep from getting caught, and work on the plans for what to do after the populace stops being drugged and wakes up."

She glanced around the group and was gratified that not one of them confessed that Anton's shuttle was not fitted with a rift generator, so was incapable of travel to Chris's home world. They would tell Chris about that and the fact that her brother was probably already dead after humanity was freed from their bondage.

We all have our sacrifices, she thought.

*****

Had Jeremy Springs not started his day on Earth with a reasonably good chance of engaging in sexual congress with a bikini-clad girl then been abducted by men on flying snowmobiles and taken across space to an alien world, when he saw what was coming out of the tree line he would have stood rooted in disbelieving incomprehension. As it was, he turned and ran with the other seven guys.

Lumbering out of the trees were three giant black scorpions. Their bodies were the size of coffee tables, their legs stretched out the width of a truck, and their tails towered over Jeremy's head. Their claws were like chainsaws. The scorpions started to pursue them, black legs scuttling and stabbing into the soft sand.

Within seconds he and the other seven newcomers had blown past the five wild men and were pelting as fast as they could down the beach. The group of five wild men laughed uproariously.

"You better pace yourselves," they hooted after the panicked group of newcomers. Jeremy fought against his instinct to run and slowed his pace like the experienced wild men, as did a few of the new group. The rest sprinted on.

"How long do we run?" Jeremy panted, glad that he had just completed weeks of Marine basic training.

The wild men did not appear in any hurry to engage in conversation. They chugged along at a slow jog, barely gaining distance from the pursuing scorpions. Before long, they came across the other seven newcomers, sitting in the hot sand gasping for breath in the heat. When the slower-paced group passed them, they staggered to their feet again and struggled to keep up. One of them, Jeremy noted with a pang of indecision, was hefty and obviously out of shape. He only ran a little while before collapsing in the sand, clutching his calf.

"Help me!" he wailed, eyes white-rimmed with panic.

Jeremy stopped and turned back, but one of the wild men called over his shoulder, "You can't help him. If you try, neither of you will make it."

Jeremy looked at the steadily approaching giant scorpions and realized that the wild man was right. He considered trying to distract the scorpions away from the fallen man but knew that the beasts would fixate on the sure meat. He started jogging backwards.

"Get up!" he bellowed. "You can do this! Just pace yourself!"

The overweight newcomer was frozen with fear and could only stare at the approaching monsters. Within seconds they were upon him. Jeremy turned away, head bowed, when the screaming started in earnest.

He walked straight into the chest of one of the wild men. They stood in a loose group, panting softly.

"*That* is when you can stop running," the tallest one said.

Jeremy regarded him coldly.

"But if everyone can remember to move just faster than them without wearing themselves out, then you just put enough distance between them and you so that when you duck back into the woods you can get out of their sight down one of the side paths so that they quit following you. Until the next one spots you, that is."

The other newcomers were gasping for breath, staring back towards the unfortunate victim who was being loudly devoured. One of them vomited.

"Why don't you fight them? Kill them? We're human fucking beings," Jeremy accused.

"Oh, we've tried it," said the tall wild man, starting back towards the woods in a more leisurely pace. "Nothing gets past those hard shells."

"Bullshit," said Jeremy, following him. "What about spears? Clubs?"?

"No metal. No hard wood, even. We just have pithy plants and palm trees. We've tried shells, coral...shit, even the rocks at the cliff are crumbly." The rest of the remaining newcomers tagged along a few paces behind them, while the four other hairy veterans scattered towards the forest at different entry points.

Jeremy considered the tall wild man carefully. The man was talking to him for the time being, and he decided to wring as much information out of him that he could before the man got frustrated, bored, or threatened by his greenhornery. He thought it best to pander to the man's sense of expertise.

"What is your name?" Jeremy asked.

"It doesn't matter here," the man answered, "but you can call me Ang 10."

"You must be a surfer," Jeremy joked. The man regarded him incomprehensibly.

"I learned not to get too familiar with newcomers like you," Ang said with a sneer. "Most of you are gone by the next morning."

"Well, Ang 10 my new friend, I'm not going to get eaten, if I can help it. Why don't you let me know what I need to know to avoid that?

Ang started jogging again towards the woods that lay beyond the wide swath of beach. The other newcomers groaned and ran along behind. Jeremy was able to keep up easily, thanks to his training. The rest were not.

Ang jogged down the maze of sandy trails between the brush, seeming to keep watch for scorpions. Occasionally he stooped to pick up various fruit that had fallen to the ground from various bushes. Jeremy copied him.

"Not the green ones," Ang muttered, "they give you bellyache and the runs, and the bugs have an easy time chasing you down."

Jeremy dropped the green one.

By this time, the other newcomers had dropped off, one by one, to seek their own way in the maze of paths. Occasionally, they ran across another scorpion, but Jeremy learned from Ang that one merely needed to dash off down a different path before the scorpion got too close.

There were streams for water. "Drink fast and keep looking around, the bugs use the creeks for ambushes," Ang instructed.

Jeremy sensed mid-afternoon that Ang was growing impatient with his presence.

"Hey, thanks for letting me tag along for a while," he said during a pause in their relentless movement. "Is there anything else important to know before we part ways?"

Ang rubbed his stubbled chin with a grubby hand, eyes constantly roving.

"At night, hole up in the middle of the biggest thorn bush you can find. If you hear them trying to get at you, make a break from the other side if you think they can reach you. Make sure you can get out of the bushes from several directions or they'll box you in there and wait you out. They can live a lot longer without food and water than we can."

Jeremy nodded. "Thanks, man."

Ang trotted away. "And stay away from the Treehouse people—

they'll eat you too," he called over his shoulder before he disappeared around a bend.

"What? Treehouse people?" Jeremy called after him, but he was gone.

For the second time that day, Jeremy was struck with the realization that he was on an alien world. This time, however, he was also aware that they were just the latest crop of victims for feeding the giant scorpions, like a mouse dropped into a snake cage. He was expected to be eaten before long, unless he ended up like the wild men, forever running for his life.

He stood regarding the sandy path through the woods before him, and a wave of depression passed over him.

"I'm going to die," he thought. He mulled that thought over and over, growing more despairing. "I'm in the valley of the shadow now."

He imagined a giant scorpion down the path from him, coming his way. He toyed with the idea of just letting it eat him, to get it over with.

"Hell with that," he thought. "I have to get back to wherever Chris is and get us out of this place."

He steeled his resolve and strode off down the path.

Before long, he found out what Ang 10 was talking about when he mentioned the "Treehouse people."

He saw a woman, in rags with long bird's-nest hair, collecting fruit. What really caught Jeremy's eye, however, was that she was carrying a basket, woven of sticks with some kind of natural cordage. She saw him, hesitated for a moment, then fled.

Jeremy gave chase. He wanted the cordage on that basket. Cordage meant tools, which meant weapons.

He was unable to gain much distance on her, and within a minute she was running up a wooden ramp into a wooden walkway among the lower branches of the trees. Jeremy did not hesitate—he started up the ramp after her.

At the top of the ramp, the woman pulled on the ends of the cords holding up the ramp, and it fell to the ground, Jeremy along with it.

He fell into the soft sand, uninjured, and immediately regained his feet. The woman was on the wooden walkway above, out of reach, regarding him.

"Leave me alone," she scolded. "If you don't get out of here I'll call the men and they'll come and kill you and eat you."

Jeremy regarded her with a wolfish grin. "Don't worry, I don't want you or your fruit. I just want the cordage."

She glowered at him. "We worked hard to make that. Leave it be."

He started untying the cordage from the wooden walkway.

"What do you want that for?" she asked, growing curious.

"I'm going to make something to kill those scorpions with."

She sat cross-legged and started eating a piece of fruit.

Jeremy recovered several long lengths of cordage, which had been twisted from some kind of plant fibers. It was strong and pliable.

"You can't kill them. There is nothing hard enough to get through their hides."

"I bet there is," said Jeremy, looking up at her. His eyes followed the wooden walkway, which connected to other walkways and platforms. Other ragged people had noticed them and started moving their way.

Jeremy recalled Ang's and the woman's warnings about their cannibalism and decided it was time to go.

"Thanks for the rope," he said, then winked and trotted off down another path. He now had the scorpions and the tree house people to avoid.

It was growing late in the afternoon. Jeremy decided to find as large a thorn bush patch as he could, like Ang 10 had advised. Before too long, he found one, with several narrow tunnels leading in from several directions into a central hollowed-out area. It appeared that it had been intentionally burrowed out by other humans in the past. Jeremy wiggled in on his belly through the thorns. He wondered whether any other wild people would join him that night, but none came. Perhaps they had been eaten long ago, either by the scorpions or the tree house people. The sand was soft, so he dug it into as comfortable a bed as he could. He longed to brush his teeth. He sniffed his armpit, but the deodorant was still holding up for now. It had only been that morning that he had woken up on Earth, he realized. He could still faintly smell the coconut of his sunscreen. He wondered how long it would take him to fully revert to wild-man status.

The night passed fitfully; he could not sleep very well. Every rustle of the foliage he imagined to be a giant scorpion trying to get to him.

Or maybe this hollowed out area is a trap set by the Treehouse People for fresh meat....

In spite of not being able to sleep deeply, he was able to will himself to rest. He remembered doing the same in boot camp, when the rumors were that the drill instructors were going to wake them in the middle of the night for forced marches and PT.

Morning came, and Jeremy woke to find his body had been feasted on by sand fleas in the night instead of cannibals. He crawled cautiously out of his thorn hive and foraged for some fruit. He craved protein and decided to try his luck on the beach for shellfish or crab. He gathered his coil of cordage and strode off towards the shore.

The beach was three or four hundred yards away from the woods. He walked along the shore, looking for the jets of clams or anything else he could forage, keeping an eye on the woods for movement that would indicate a giant scorpion.

He found a dead crab, and sniffed it hopefully. It appeared fresh enough, so he tore into it hungrily, cutting his hand on the jagged shell. There was not much meat, but he ate it gratefully. Jeremy looked at the cut on his hand, then at the crab shell. It dawned on him that this might be dense enough to pierce scorpion shell, but realized that it was nowhere near large enough to use for that purpose. That line of thought trailed away as he continued his solitary journey along the pounding surf.

An hour later, his vigilance in looking out for scorpions was rewarded. He saw the dark shape of one far ahead of him on the beach, and realized that he would have to retreat to the woods. He started towards the tree line, glancing over his shoulder periodically to see if the scorpion would give chase. It did not.

In fact, Jeremy noticed with growing curiosity, the scorpion had not moved. He stopped, peering towards the animal, trying to see what it was up to. Was it digging for clams? Jeremy wondered if he could scavenge a meal from whatever the scorpion had stirred up.

He inched closer. The scorpion remained motionless. Jeremy approached within twenty yards, then ten. He realized that there were flies buzzing around the beast. With a flood of relief, he realized that it was dead.

His first thought was of eating...he wondered if there was any good meat on this carcass. He imagined tasting a giant lobster, but the overwhelming stench that assaulted him when he got close cured him of that ambition. He was about to leave, when he remembered his cut hand and the crab shell. A possibility crept into his mind. He located the huge stinger at the back of the segmented tail. It was the perfect size to affix to the end of a shaft as an axe. It was very sharp, black, and hard as obsidian. He broke it off, with some difficulty.

Jeremy considered the rest of the carcass. He eyed the sharp segments at the end of the scorpion's legs, and broke off several of them for use as spear heads or axe hafts. They, too, were quite sharp.

Jeremy walked slowly back towards the trees, with the stinger, legs, and cordage; components for his weaponry.

"This," he thought, "is a game-changer."

*****

Ron Golden and Jack Strong chased the gnomes down the mountain. At first, they were able to keep them in sight, but the gnomes quickly gained on them and did not seem to need rest. Soon Ron and Strong were bent over with heaving chests, hands on knees, while the gnomes got farther and farther ahead. Soon they only caught glimpses of their red hats through the rocks and tree trunks far ahead. They jogged after the gnomes when they caught their breaths again, but they were gone.

"We could just follow their tracks," Strong suggested hopefully.

"Do you know anything about tracking?" Ron replied sourly.

Strong could only shrug.

"If only Smithson were along. He knows how to do stuff like that," Ron sighed, hands on hips.

They actually did find some small footprints after looking carefully for them, and followed them for some time downhill through the woods. After an hour, the ground started to level out more, and the trees started to thin out. The ground became more rocky and the trail harder to follow. Soon the trees thinned out completely, and they found themselves at the top of a rocky slope overlooking a vast wasteland.

The skies were a dusty brown, and it was hot. The terrain was flat, with random patterns of scrubby vegetation. Dark streaks could have been shadows or ravines. Far across the plain, they noticed a dust devil spinning disjointedly towards them. The wind scoured the ground clean of any tracks.

"Shit," Strong said simply.

They stood at the top of the slope, trying to formulate a plan.

"We could just set out in a straight line and keep looking," said Ron, "but if they are going at another angle, every step we take will be getting farther and farther from them."

"That, and we have no idea where they are heading for," said Strong, shaking his head. "Sacred Mountain my ass."

"The Sacred Gnome Mountain is straight that way," said a gravelly voice nearby. Ron and Jack nearly jumped out of their skins and swiveled their heads looking for the source of the voice.

Sitting with their backs to a large rock nearby were two figures, one short, one tall. They were dressed in cloaks that were colored the same as the rock, which explained why Ron and Strong did not see them at first. The smaller one was stocky, with long hair and a long, bushy, brown beard. His face was heavily lined, and his eyes glowed like black coals from under bushy brows. His gnarled, strong hand rested on the head of a huge, double-bladed axe.

The taller of the two was fair-skinned and fair-haired, with refined, handsome features. His ears were slightly pointed. The feathered ends of several arrows extended from what must have been a quiver at his back.

Ron and Strong stared stupidly at them for several long seconds.

"An elf and a dwarf traveling together?" whispered Strong.

"You have read us," said the taller one with a smile, and stood. "What work are you from?"

Ron and Jack exchanged glances.

"What *work* are we from?" Ron asked.

It was the elf and the dwarf's turn to exchange glances.

"You are not from here," said the dwarf. "Are you begotten?"

"That is the second time I've heard that term since we've come here," said Ron. "What does it mean?"

The elf's eyes narrowed. "Where are you from? How did you get here? Are you dead or dreaming or did you come through magic?"

Ron debated telling him momentarily, but realized at the moment he had nothing to lose. "We are from Earth. We came here using a...a device that allows us to travel from there to other times and places."

"Ahhh...," said the dwarf. "Technology then. And did the wee gnomes steal your machine?"

"Well, the part that makes it work," said Ron. "Did you see which way they went?"

"You will have great difficulty catching them," said the elf. "They struck out straight across the Dream Plains."

Ron and Strong exchanged glances. "Are those the Dream Plains?" Strong asked, waving his hand at the dusty wasteland.

"Yesss...," said the elf confusedly. "You do not know the Dream Plains?"

"They have no idea where they are," said the dwarf with dawning realization.

"How did they decide to come here, then?" the elf asked him.

"It must have been by mistake. I don't think they had any idea what this place is," the dwarf answered.

"How about you educate us, then," Ron said.

The elf and the dwarf exchanged glances.

"You tell them," said the dwarf. "I have no tongue for such things."

The elf rubbed his chin, looking for somewhere to begin.

"Your world," he said after a long pause, "is quite different from here."

He said nothing for some time. Ron wondered if he was waiting for a question.

"Well *that* was eloquent," growled the dwarf. "Look, this world was made through the power of awareness collapsing the quantum uncertainty, the wave function, the fuzzy nothingness until something observes it, see? In your world it is done jointly—
you could say *co-created* between living beings and their Creator. Here it is made only by the created beings, the sentient awarenesses, either through intentional creation or random dreaming."

Ron and Strong stood blinking at him.

"I'll try to be plainer," the dwarf continued. "You know how nothing exists as anything other than a quantum uncertainty cloud until it is observed?"

"Where is Professor LaGrue when we need him?" whispered Strong.

"Let's assume we have heard these principles long ago and do not remember them," said Ron.

The dwarf munched his beard with frustration.

"Allow me," interrupted the elf. "In your world, assuming nothing exists unless a consciousness observes it, does the moon disappear if nobody is looking at it? Some of your scientists would say 'yes,' but those are either the outer fringe or cranks. It doesn't disappear, of course, but it is not because there is no consciousness collapsing the wave function. There is *always* a consciousness there to collapse the wave function and bring things into being—if not a human being or other living thing, then God is there to do it. He is infinitely aware in your world, down to the farthest star or tiniest grain of sand. But not so here. We are made by the imaginations of humans and only continue to exist as long as some other human is reading, watching, or remembering us."

"You mean, you are actually just book characters?" asked Strong.

"Yes," said the dwarf. "We are *made*, by a writer, and continue to live beyond him because others continue to read him. Others who are made will fade to oblivion when they are forgotten. We are among the lucky who are able to roam this world and travel to other lands from other creations and meet other Made."

"You mean," said Strong, "that not only are you characters from books here, but the worlds from those books too?"

"Of course," said the elf. "But that map eventually changes too: As those memories fade, the lands fade too. Maps are in constant need of revision around here. Not only because of memories, but the architecture of the place. You'll see."

"So," said Strong, waving his hand across the plain, "out there somewhere is Middle-earth? Old England with King Arthur? Sherlock Holmes's London? Atlantis? And up there are Star Treks and Star Wars? Are they all here? With all their characters?"

"Yes," said the elf. "All here, laid out, like a vast, interconnected map. Even the 'dead' characters are still around as long as someone is still actively reading or watching or remembering them."

"Why would they call this 'Hell?'" railed Strong.

The elf and the dwarf exchanged troubled glances.

"Think about it, laddie," the dwarf said quietly. "There is no hint of God here. When we fade, we are gone forever. And not only that, we were created by fallible humans; not only is there monstrous evil here in their creations, but whatever good there is can only be what their human creators can imperfectly make. Whereas you, you begotten of other living God-created beings, are parts of that glorious whole! You don't realize your fortune."

"I thought Hell was some place that bad people's souls go to after they die," pondered Ron.

"Oh it is," said the elf. "But not as disembodied ghosts. And the whole punishment for eternity in a lake of fire business is way over there to the East many days journey. Disembodied ghosts don't have nerves to suffer pain with, right? But Hell is bigger than that. It takes those souls a while to figure out they can just walk out of that part of it. If a Begotten is so wrapped up in themselves that they create their own little world instead of living in the real one, then that is usually where they choose to remain after they die. They don't realize that whatever worlds that they or others create cannot possibly compare with the ones that God made. But people don't just come here after they die. You all die little deaths every night and create little worlds in your dreams. Hence the Dream Plains," the elf said, pointing across the brown, whirlwind-full plains.

Ron gazed across the vast plains and the little dust devils that crossed them.

"You mean," he said, "that those little tornadoes are dreaming people?"

The dwarf nodded. "Yes. If you cross the plains in search of your wee gnomes, try to avoid them. You get caught up in whatever dream the dreamer is having. Some are nice, some are not."

"The gnomes!" Ron remembered, slapping his forehead. "Where did you say they went? And who the hell are they?"

"They have been here since the beginning, when God sundered Hell from the original world line. They have their purpose. Their Sacred Mountain is across the plains in that direction. If you cross straight through," he said, drawing a line in the dirt with the toe of his boot, "in that direction, *without veering even a wee bit*, you'll hit it. If you wander off to the right even a little, you'll hit 20th Century Subdivision Land. Off to the left and you'll run smack into Pornlandia."

"Pornlandia?" mused Strong, eyebrow rising.

"Believe me," said the elf, "you don't want to get stuck there."

Ron and Strong stood quietly, not knowing what to say.

"Well, good luck tracking them down," the dwarf offered.

"Hey, you two feel like coming along? Helping us?" Ron asked hopefully.

"Yeah, you have a lot of experience tracking," added Strong, hoping to make points for remembering their book.

The elf and dwarf chuckled uncomfortably. "No thanks," the elf said. "We're on our own path."

"Right. Started at the caves and have lots more of the worlds to see," added the dwarf. "We're off to see Arrakis. Here, you might need this," he added, reaching into his belt behind his back. He produced a small futuristic-looking gun and handed it over to Ron, grip first.

"Careful, there, laddie!" the dwarf said. "That thing packs a punch. It's from a Man in Black. Had to trade a variable sword for it."

Strong's eyes widened. "Wow, thanks!"

"Good luck to you," said the elf, and the two of them walked resolutely off in the direction Ron and Strong had come from.

"I have a feeling we will wish we did a better job of convincing them to come along and help us," Ron mused, looking across the dusty plains with the brown skies. There were now more whirlwinds, they noticed, that came and went. Some lasted only a brief time; others took several minutes to disperse.

They looked carefully at the arrow the dwarf had drawn with his foot and tried to find some landmark across the plains that they could aim for, but there was nothing that they could discern in that direction but more brown sky. They decided to strike out across the plain as best they could and look for a landmark that they could work their way towards as soon as possible.

They were already tired when they started. The dusty ground was hard going, and occasionally they ran into deep ravines that had to be circumvented. Once on the other side, they made their best guess as to what direction they had been traveling, but Ron had a sinking suspicion that they were making a hash of it. After several ravines, he also began to suspect that Strong was intentionally angling towards Pornlandia.

It was after three hours of this that the first whirlwind overcame them. It came suddenly from behind Ron, forming out of nowhere. Before he could react, he felt a rush of wind, and found himself in a room with wooden, curved walls and plank floors. It was lit by a gas lantern, and the floor swayed and rocked. He realized he was on a sailing ship of some kind. The edges of the room faded in and out of blackness, like dreams do. He was not alone. Sitting in an elaborate animal skin and metal framed chair was a tall, thin man, with incredibly long arms and legs. His head was massive, covered with a matted black beard, flecked with foam and spittle. The man's eye sockets were empty, and a rattling, wet exhalation coughed up from somewhere within the beard. Ron felt that the eyeless sockets somehow sensed him, and were scanning the room for him. A pointed, pale tongue began worming its way out of the beard.

Ron realized with a visceral shock that it wasn't a tongue, but some kind of suckered tentacle. The tentacle disappeared into the hole in the beard, then a black, tarry substance began to ooze out of it. Ron was engulfed in dread, then a hand grabbed him. He screamed, then was pulled out of the dream by Strong.

"Whoa, almost lost you there, pardner. Didn't want to jump in there, looked bad."

"Thanks," said Ron, getting his bearings back. "Must try to avoid those things," he said shakily.

Less than five minutes later, however, another dream whirlwind took them both by surprise. Ron and Strong found themselves next to a large, hairy man who was relieving himself against a stone wall. Torrents of urine coursed from the man, while he moaned loudly, head back, eyes rolled back in their sockets. They were both overcome with the irresistible urge to pee as well and fumbled their pants open in haste to join him. They peed for what seemed like an eternity, then were deposited out of the dream back onto the dusty plain. They were both covered with urine.

"Goddamn it," said Strong. They did the best they could to clean themselves by rubbing dust on their clothes.

"What the hell was that?" wondered Ron out loud.

"Probably some dude who had been sleeping a long time and had to go. I've had a dream like that," mused Strong.

"So if that was a dream, then why did we actually piss ourselves?" asked Ron.

Strong considered this with growing concern.

"I guess while in the dream we have physical effects of what is going on in that dream."

They both mulled over the ramifications of this.

"Well, we have to do better at avoiding them. I've had lots of violent dreams," said Strong.

"I still don't remember most of mine," said Ron.

"That doesn't mean you are not having them. They are probably either too mundane or horrible to remember. Let's get out of here as fast as we can."

They looked around and realized with a sinking feeling that they had no idea where the dream had deposited them and which direction they had been going.

"Shit. Now what?"

Ron pursed his lips with a sour face. "No idea. No sun, moon, stars, no landmarks, no footprints. We may as well pick a direction at random. Once we get off the plain, we'll ask where Pornlandia is and go that way along the edge of the plain. I'm sure everyone will know where that is."

They picked a direction and started out.

They were able to travel three hours, dodging whirlwinds, before another one caught Strong from behind. Ron was able to stay on the perimeter, reach in and grab Strong by the arm rather quickly. Strong was shuddering when he came out.

"I won't ask," said Ron.

"Yeah, don't. It was a fat woman. Who must have been a big fan of oral sex." He paused and shook his head in an attempt to clear it. "Yeah, I think I know what the elf meant by not wanting to go through Pornlandia."

They trudged on, warily, across the Dream Plains. It occurred to Ron, like ice water in his veins, they might be there for a long time. If not forever.

—5—

Tracey waited. The police arrived, and checked the house for Maurice, but he was gone, of course. Tracey did not tell them that Maurice had just left. They insisted on keeping an officer in the house in case Maurice showed up as promised. It took them two days to agree to leave, instructing Tracey to call if she had the least hint that Maurice was around. Not many people had simply vanished from the King County Jail like that. They continued investigating Ron's disappearance, but quickly ran out of leads. When someone isn't even in the same universe, there are no tracks to follow.

Chris and Jeremy's disappearances were also being independently investigated, but none of the agencies involved knew that there were two others who had gone missing. Tracey was in no hurry to inform them; it would have just ratcheted up the complications exponentially. She knew that they would eventually find out, but decided, with no support or evidence whatsoever, that she would resolve the situation before that happened.

After four days of woodenly plodding through her daily routines, the dream that Maurice had predicted came.

She rolled over in her sleep at three in the morning and her eyes fluttered open, sensing movement in the room. She sat bolt upright, and saw an odd, translucent green, cylinder-shaped creature with undulating hair all along it, floating gently in the air near the door.

"Oh, a Flying Pickle," she thought, and with that memory all the other memories came flooding back by themselves: the Underground base near the Denver Airport, the Mods and "Space Command" people, Bodie, the rift, the Sea Tribes, the Dive with Bell the Oceanic, Maurice and Leonard, Eiffelia and her Stripes. She even remembered the life as the wife of the richest man in the world and its evaporation into the amalgam of the old world as it would have been had they never traveled through the rift.

One moment her life had been limited, the next it was as though the veil had been lifted and her fuller, more experienced Self had replaced her. She realized how Ron must have seen things all along.

She stood there, wide-eyed, until the Flying Pickle left the room. She knew she had to follow it.

It floated down the hall into the living room and through the front door as if it wasn't there. She followed, wondered briefly whether she should change out of her pajamas. By the time she opened the front door, it was already a good ways down the street. She hurried after it, afraid to lose track, not even locking the front door.

She was able to run along the grass of adjacent yards only so long; soon she was forced onto the paved streets. The gravel dug into her bare feet and was painful. She paused, wondering if she should run back to the house to find some shoes, but was afraid that the Flying Pickle would not wait for her. She chased after it, as fast as her tender feet could carry her.

The Flying Pickle ducked down an alleyway between two house's back yard fences, and she followed, stirring a dog into frenzied barking. An overhanging blackberry vine caught her momentarily, and she almost lost sight of her quarry. Tracey pulled herself free, tearing her pajama sleeve, and emerged onto a sidewalk on a busy street. She saw the creature half a block away to the South. She followed, passing a convenience store and a closed strip mall.

Pain shot from her left foot: She looked down with a stifled cry and saw that she had stepped on glass shards from a broken bottle. Blood gushed from her foot. With a curse, she saw the Flying Pickle getting farther away. Steeling herself against the pain, she limped after it, leaving red footprints on the sidewalk.

The Flying Pickle made several more turns, taking her farther away from known areas. She lost track even of what part of town she was in.

Tracey thought she was gaining on it, but it took an abrupt right turn into a neon-lit doorway and vanished.

She hurried up to the building where the door was and read the neon sign in the large plate-glass window: "House of Kong Chinese Restaurant." Another neon sign, this one in blinking red and yellow with a stylized martini glass, read "Lounge."

She pushed her way into the shabby, dimly-lit restaurant, and glanced around for the Flying Pickle. It was nowhere to be seen.

A Chinese woman sat behind a counter with a cash register, with folded takeout menus in a pile. A torn paper lantern hung behind, showing the dim bulb inside. There was an opening to the lounge area, with jukebox music and garishly-colored light leaching from it, and a mostly empty restaurant area. The carpet was thin and sticky against her bare feet, and the heavy smell of broken oil and five spice was in the air. Tracey noticed that the Chinese woman was eyeing her bloody foot with obvious ire.

"Where did it go?" Tracey asked with urgency.

"You can't come in here like that. You leave," the Chinese woman scolded.

"No, I have to find where that...there was a...it looked like a green glassy cucumber with little hairs all over it—it flew in here," she mumbled.

The Chinese woman shook her head. "No flying green thing. You go."

Tracey took stock of what she looked like: torn pajamas, sweat-plastered hair, bloody foot. She felt the overwhelming urge to burst into tears, but it passed quickly, leaving a dead calm, tinged with desperate denial.

"No, I need to find that Flying Pickle," she said flatly. "Or," she added as an afterthought, "is this where Andrew Morrow is?"

The woman regarded her a little too off-handedly. "No Andrew Morrow. No Flying Pickle. Go away now."

Tracey folded her arms across her chest. "I want to see Andrew Morrow. I'm not leaving until I do."

The Chinese woman stared at her coldly for a long moment, then picked up the phone behind the counter, dialed it, and spoke into it briefly. Tracey had a moment of elated triumph that lasted only a second.

"Police on the way now, you better go," said the woman.

Tracey felt deflated, but had nothing to lose now. She stood her ground.

Long minutes passed, while the two of them regarded each other.

"Police coming. Any minute now."

"I'll wait," Tracey answered.

She waited.

"Can I be of some assistance?" said a voice behind her. Tracey turned, and was face to face with a rather obese Asian man in a black and white Yukata with a bamboo pattern. His hair, on the rotund head, was short-cropped. He wore circular framed glasses that hid eyes deeply set in the fleshy eye sockets. His mouth was slightly parted.

"I'm here to see Andrew Morrow," Tracey said curtly.

"I am Andrew Morrow, at your service," the man said.

"Oh," said Tracey, "I was expecting...."

"A Caucasian man?" he finished for her. "I have an English name and a Hawaiian body," he smiled. "I am glad you finally found me. Maurice said that you would come looking."

She stood regarding him, not knowing what to say.

"Would you like to come up?" he invited.

She nodded. He bowed to the Chinese woman behind the counter, then led her through the alcove between the restaurant and bar areas to a door that she had assumed was a broom closet. He opened it, revealing a staircase leading up. Morrow gestured to her to ascend, which she did.

The stairs were solid stone, which seemed out of place with the construction of the restaurant, and were cold against her bare feet.

"Sorry, I'm bleeding all over your stairs," she said feebly.

"Don't worry about that," he said, with a dismissive wave as he climbed behind her.

She emerged at the top of the stairs and was shocked. The room was much bigger than the entire restaurant below, with stone walls and huge wooden beams supporting a vaulted roof. Heavy wooden shelves lined the walls, filled with antique books, rocks, animal bones, and other mysterious artifacts. There were several large picture windows which looked out on incongruous exteriors: one showed a mountain slope at dusk; another looked into a dark forest at daytime, a third showed a rocky coastline at night, and a fourth appeared to be looking into deep space. Tracey at first assumed that they were merely extremely realistic back-lit light-boxes, but then realized that they were not. Doorways led off into other chambers of unguessed size and scope.

"Is this one of those places like the garden or the floor between floors that the Mods keep? One of those 'bigger on the inside than outside' places?"

There was a stone table, with overstuffed chairs. Morrow smiled, motioned her to be seated, and took one of the chairs himself. He sat for a moment regarding her, fingers templed. She did not know what to say, where to begin.

"Would you like some tea?" he said finally. She nodded gratefully.

Morrow rang a little bell that he picked up from a side table, and a strange little person appeared. He was small, bent, and almost looked like a wizened monkey. Tracey looked more closely, without meaning to be rude, and thought that it might actually *be* a monkey.

"Some tea, please," Morrow said. The monkey man disappeared, and returned before long with a tray bearing a porcelain pot and two cups and saucers. He poured, asked her with his eyes whether she took cream or sugar. She shook he head and thanked him.

When they were seated back in their chairs, the strangeness of the situation, the cold of the night, and her exertion finally caught up with Tracey and she began to shake uncontrollably.

Morrow called for a blanket, and the monkey man brought one and draped her with it. He returned again with a basin of water and slippers, and bathed and dressed her wounded foot.

Soon, Tracey felt much better and more comfortable.

"Maurice said that you are not a human being," she said eventually.

He barked a laugh. "He's one to talk."

He didn't seem to be in any rush to say anything else on the matter, but Tracey decided to push the issue.

"I don't mean to be rude, I would like to know what you *are*, if not human. You look like someone playing at being a human being or wearing a human mask badly." She was reminded of Mr. Stone and Ms. Lake, who also had that air about them.

"Ah, I must try to do better. Well, if we can't proceed without getting this out of the way, let me tell you my tale."

Tracey sipped her tea, and scrunched further into her blanket. Morrow sat for a moment, collecting his thoughts, then let forth a great sigh.

"I suppose I should begin at the beginning. You are, I believe, familiar with Eiffelia."

"We have met," Tracey frowned.

"Yes, good work getting rid of her among the Tribes."

Tracey narrowed her eyes. "How do you know about that? I only just now remembered it happened at all."

Morrow smiled. "I have a method of seeing many things, in many places and times."

"Maurice mentioned that I should ask you about that...I can't remember what he called it. Something-orium."

Morrow raised his eyebrow. "Something-orium? What kind of 'orium?'"

Tracey shrugged helplessly.

"A vomitorium?" he suggested. Tracey stifled a giggle, shook her head.

"A valedictorian? A moratorium?"

She shook her head, trying to remember. She knew Morrow knew exactly what she was talking about and it annoyed her that he was playing dumb.

"Crematorium? *Sanatorium?*"

"It did start with an 's,'" she offered.

"He must mean my Scrytorium."

"That was it," Tracey confirmed, pointing her finger. "What is that anyway?"

"Like I said, a manner to see many things. All in good time. First, though, my tale. You know of Eiffelia, but Ron had a more intimate experience with her. This is his fate, and fortunately less so with me and you. Ron observed her being fed in the trench by giant scorpions."

"I did not know that," she said, brows furrowing. "Giant scorpions?"

"Yes, a holdover that she kept from her old prehistoric days. More recently, your son Jeremy had some dealings with them on her home planet of Cambria."

"What kind of dealings? Is he safe?"

"Yes, for the moment. So is Chris. But we will discuss them later. Now we need to talk about the giant scorpions."

Tracey forced herself to patience in hearing about her children later.

"Sounds like you have had some dealings with them yourself," she managed.

"You could say that. I used to be one."

"Excuse me?"

"Yes, you heard that correctly. I began my existence as a little tiny baby giant scorpion, bred for millions of years for the purpose of serving Eiffelia. On the Earth you visited, before you managed to wipe it clean of her, we stuffed meat into her pores. On Cambria we did the same but also ran around on the land harvesting the excess human beings. In days past, when she warred with other sponges, my kind served as her armies against her rival sponges.

My job was one of the beach enforcers, like Jeremy had to face. I was gone years before he got there, though. Once I was fully grown, we chased ragged people around on the beach at the base of a giant cliff, and ate what we caught. Every now and then, a new batch of criminals or unwanted and unneeded people would be dumped on the beach; we would gorge on the weak of body or mind, and the rest would join the other ragged people to be picked off later."

"That is horrible."

"Did you expect anything better from Eiffelia? Well anyway, one fine, sunny morning we saw the transport gliding over the trees and hurried down to the beach where they offloaded the meat. There were four of us and ten new victims. They lost no time running away for the beach or the trees once they saw us. We scorpions gave chase, of course. I remember one of them caught my eye, though: He ran slowly, straight along the beach. That intrigued me, since only the ragged pack who lived around there did that. So I chased after him. We ran along the beach for a while, then he did something that really confused me. He started to sing."

"Sing?"

"Yes. It was the damndest thing. I had never heard music, of course, and had no idea what he was doing. But there he went, singing while running for his life along the beach. I was intrigued. So instead of eating him I captured him and put him in a cave."

"That was nice of you."

"Nice didn't enter into it. I just wanted to see what this noise was all about before I ate him. And I had to keep the other scorpions off of him in the meantime. I didn't have to lock him into the cave, either; the other scorpions lurking around in the brush was enough to keep him trapped in there."

"So what happened?"

"He kept singing. Hymns, it turned out. Well in spite of being lowly giant arachnids, we had evolved a rudimentary intelligence and could communicate with each other through a vocabulary of hisses. After a while of listening to the old guy, I started hissing along with him. He heard that and actually encouraged me. Eventually, he taught me to speak in a hissing kind of voice."

"Wow. And what did you guys talk about?"

"Not much, at first. And it started looking like there wasn't going to be any long-term talking either, since he wouldn't eat any of the human meat I brought him, and the fruit he would eat wasn't enough to sustain him long-term. Water was difficult. We sang, him in his reedy little weak voice and me hissing. No danger of making the pop charts!"

He paused, wistfully remembering. Tracy remained quiet.

"Anyway, he told me that he was part of an order and showed me a trident. He wasn't afraid of dying, said that he would continue on between the bubbles and be with God in the real world. I asked him if he was angry that he had been put in this predicament. He said no, that hardship and suffering were all just part of the grand story, and that stories would be boring and pointless without them. He said that was why we chose to be here. Eventually he got sicker and sicker and begged me to eat him."

Tracey raised her eyebrows. "You didn't!"

"I'm afraid I did. It ended his suffering, and I didn't want the others to get to him. It didn't seem right."

Tracey didn't know what to say.

"So anyway, the other scorpions moved on, disappointed. I lingered around the cave for a few days, when the most remarkable thing happened."

Tracey raised an eyebrow, sipping tea.

"Some people came. There were two of them, a man and a woman. They weren't like the other miserable victims; they came walking up instead of running for their lives. They were dressed in odd clothes, not rags or papery coveralls like the other humans. I assumed they must have come in their own ship. At first I was afraid that they had come looking for the old man to rescue him, and they might be angry or attack me when they found him gone. But they just stood at the mouth of the cave and looked at me.

"After a while I realized that they weren't angry. I told them, in my hissy little voice, that he was gone. And then they said the damnedest thing. 'We aren't here for him. We're here for you.'

"And then an even stranger thing happened. Water came out of my eyes! Out of my glassy, black, compound eyes. I had no idea what was going on, scorpions don't cry. But there it was.

"'What is wrong?' they asked.

"'I feel terrible,' I said, 'because he is dead.' I didn't want to admit that I ate him. I was still a little afraid.

"'Where is his body?' they asked me. I didn't know what to say, so I just writhed a little, clawing the ground. They didn't say anything; they were just waiting for me. After a while, the silence became unbearable. So I started to hiss out a hymn we used to sing together. 'Amaaa..zing Graaa...ce....'"

Morrow stopped, and Tracey noticed him wipe the corner of his eye. She waited for him to continue.

"So anyway, they were delighted and asked if I liked music. 'What is music?' I asked. They gave each other a knowing glance, then pulled out a little electronic device. It was a music player, I guess, among other things. Anyway, they played the hymn for real, but an instrumental version. I was shocked, because the only music I had ever heard was the old man's weak singing. I found it wondrously beautiful at the time, but this was better.

"'Do you like that?' they asked. I was speechless. So then they whispered to each other for a moment. They must have decided to really go for the jugular, because they put on Copeland's 'Appalachian Spring.'

"Of course, I had never imagined anything like that. It was the most transcendent, mind-scrambling thing that I had ever experienced. In fact, I didn't just experience it, I was transported out of myself and ceased existence for that time as a separate consciousness. By the time those little bells closed out the last of the song, I just lay there, weeping, willing to die because nothing else could ever match the beauty of that. Of course it occurred to me a few seconds later that there may be any number of other pieces of music out there.

"'You liked that?' one of them asked. They seemed surprised that I had the capacity to. 'There's more,' they said. 'Lots more.'

"I couldn't bear the thought of a vast pool of music out there that I would never experience once they left. I asked them to take me with them. They were again surprised and whispered to each other while I waited.

"'We can't take you—our ship is only configured for human beings,' they said."

He paused, sipping his tea with a half-smile.

"I can't help but notice," said Tracey, "that you are no longer a giant scorpion."

"Yes. Well, there you go."

"So how did they pull that off? Magic? Miracle? What happened to the 'Ground Rules?'"

"Yes, indeed! But we don't know them all, and sometimes when something happens that we think violates them, it is merely revealing a deeper level of the rules that we didn't know before. Which brings us to our current conundrum. Why are you here?"

"You know why I am here," she said quietly.

"Well," he answered with a wry smile, "I have an *idea* why you are here, and you have an idea why you are here. Spelling it out, however, has its own value. You see, I might have a Hawaiian body and an English name, but I have a 19th century German philosopher brain. Let's define things."

"All right," she said, placing her tea firmly on the saucer and then the table. "I want to find Ron."

"No you don't," he said. "You know exactly where he is."

She started to disagree, but then waived her hands in frustration.

"I know *vaguely* where he is. He and Strong took the rift generator and went to explore an alternate universe line and somehow got trapped there."

"That was no 'alternative universe line.' Not like the one you were in when you were the wife of the richest man in the world because his grandpa knew where the gold was and what to invest in. No, poor Ron is in Hell."

"All right then," said Tracey coolly, "if he is in 'hell,' what do you mean by that? Your turn to 'define things.' You can't possibly mean the one with lakes of fire and little red devils with pitchforks."

"Oh, those are there, of course, but only because that image is so strong and maintained by humans. There is a lot more going on there than Dante's Inferno, though, and a lot worse. We'll look in on them later. For now, though, what do you want?"

Tracey wondered why he was being such a stickler. It occurred to her that the forced formality was almost ritual-like, yet light-hearted. It occurred to her that it was similar to how Bell had acted when she was undergoing the test of the Dive.

Must be a Trident thing, she thought.

"So this is a test, isn't it?" she asked.

"You could say that," Morrow answered, with a grin. "Although not one you can fail exactly. The only way you can *fail* is if you give up. The real question is whether you will succeed or not. Only one in a thousand does. And of those that *do* succeed only one in a thousand does it quickly instead of years and years."

Tracey's heart sank.

"So are you the one-in-a-million candidate?"

"We'll see," she said flatly.

"Good answer," Morrow said with a little golf clap. "So what is it you want?"

"*Knowing* that Ron is in 'hell,' I want to get him out of there."

Morrow pursed his lips. "Well, that is impossible, you know."

"Why impossible? Ron made it there—why would it be impossible for me?"

"Because Ron had the rift generator, and you do not. Nor is there one anywhere in this universe that you can put your hands on and no way to contact anyone who does have one."

She resisted the urge to throw the teacup at him. She sat wondering what to say next. Morrow said nothing, just sat there with an inscrutable smile and half-lidded eyes. She realized he was not going to say anything; the ball was in her court. The test could be passed or failed on what she said next.

But didn't he say that I couldn't fail?

"Well I guess I need a miracle then," she said.

Morrow's smile broadened. "Exactly so," he said.

Tracey was momentarily confused. She had spoken it as an offhand comment, but Morrow appeared to have taken it as a literal answer. She held her tongue.

"So what does that mean, that you need a miracle? Let us unpack that statement, because if we understand it, I mean *really* understand it, you may have the seeds already planted that we can sprout into reality."

"Uh, ok," Tracey said, with just the ghost of an eye roll.

"Ah, we have a skeptic," Morrow said with apparent relish. "It may surprise you to hear that skepticism here is helpful. This is not one of those things that requires blind faith to make it real. I mean, things are either real or not, right? As long as doubt doesn't turn into rigid disbelief in the face of evidence and experience, it will help here, ok?"

Tracey nodded.

"Good then. So...who are you?"

"I am Tracey Springs," she said.

"Who is Tracey Springs?"

"A woman. A human being."

"And what is a human being?"

She folded her arms.

"I am a giant scorpion with a Hawaiian body with an English name with a German philosopher brain and a three-year-old's habit of annoying questions," he said. "But unless you become like a little child, you cannot enter the Kingdom of Heaven."

Tracey again wondered if his statement was literal or not.

"Look," she said, "I'm afraid I'm a little bit scientific and rational. I'm going to have a hard time believing in miracles. I have a hard time believing you were magically transformed from a giant bug into you. Just like I'm going to have a hard time believing that human beings are anything but animals that evolved intelligence and now build buildings and hang out in bars and read books and watch TV and go to work."

He nodded. "Yes, but is that *all* you are? Walking meat?"

"I have intelligence. Sentience."

"And what is that?" he asked.

"Electrical activity in my brain."

"And this is from the woman who made the Dive? Who shared consciousness with a cephalopod and an alien Flying Pickle? So what was 'Tracey Springs' while you were swimming around as a giant octopus? Or having one of your dreams, for that matter?"

She considered this quietly. Her pugilistic attitude surprised her too. She was not only surprised at her urge to argue, but that she was taking the side of materialism. While agnostic, she certainly had done her share of "spiritual seeking," including what she considered a spiritual, if not religious, experience during the Dive, as Morrow had mentioned. Morrow appeared to be making an argument for a certain worldview, taking a certain position, and she wanted him to fight for every inch of it.

"Are you going to take the position of classical physics that everything is material, including the thoughts in your head?" he asked.

She stubbornly remained silent.

"So you are going to take the two-hundred-year-old Newtonian view that sees the world as elementary particles making atoms, then molecules, then compounds, then stuff of the world, including us and our minds. You are just going to ignore quantum physics, which shows us that consciousness starts everything, and the universe flowers out of delight in itself?"

"I'm not going to deny that—I just don't get it," she said.

"Oh, I don't either: If anyone says they intuitively 'get' quantum physics, they are full of hooey," he laughed. "Consciousness collapses the wave function. Brains are part of the wave function too, and are part of the material world that is getting collapsed; they can't collapse themselves any more than the double-slit apparatus can. So it must be more than brains."

"Ok, smart guy, then answer me this: How did the wave function get collapsed before there was consciousness? Before we evolved, was the whole universe just an un-collapsed quantum state?"

"A good question," he said. "Many people wiser than we are have wondered that. If there is no observer, how did the world come into being? Did the universe simply coalesce out of nothing when we reached some arbitrary point of 'enough intelligence?' And what point was that? Can a dog's observation collapse the wave function? Can a rock's?"

"Does a dog have Buddha nature?" Tracey muttered.

"Exactly!" he said with relish. "Mu!"

"Well once again, I have no idea why you are mucking around with this when I have miracles to discover how to do."

"The point is, why does it have to be human consciousness that collapses the wave function? Even before life on Earth, even before life *anywhere*, the wave function was collapsed by consciousness. So who was it?"

"I guess you are going to say God," she answered.

"Yes, God, in collaboration with our shared Universal Consciousness, that made everything and is in everything. Atheists go to great lengths to start from the pre-supposition that *since there is no God* then the universe must have sprung out of nothing, in spite of the logical fallacy inherent therein. They use science as their religion."

"So you don't like science."

"Of course I like science. Science is great. But science should be a tool of the mind, not a frame of it. You know the whole analogy of through a glass darkly? Science is great at examining the minutia of the glass, each little pore and ripple of it, each microscopic mote of dust on the surface and the patterns they make. But it denies that there is anything beyond the glass and doesn't realize that the glass is part of a window looking out into the wide world."

She spread her hands helplessly.

"The point is," he continued, "where does this fit in with our present problem? How do you get a miracle and get Ron out of Hell? You need to start by understanding the Ground Rules, why some things are impossible and some things are not."

"Ah, the elusive Ground Rules again. Well that seems easy enough. If something is impossible, by definition it cannot be."

"Ah," he said, "but are there not levels of impossible? I mean, not by definition, but in practicality? It is one thing to say that it is impossible to have a round square, and another to say it is impossible for the Mariners to win the World Series. Or somewhere in the middle, it is impossible to walk on water, for instance. I mean, some things are 'impossible' only because we have not been able to pull them off yet."

"So how far down on the 'impossibility scale' is getting Ron and Strong out of Hell?"

"You need some way of getting them out, like one of those rift generators. So what are the chances of getting one?"

"Cornish Bob had one, and that was in this universe. But he ended up giving it to Ron, and now it is gone from it. But that doesn't mean that is the only one. Ron said he had the plans for one from his Pop, but how would we get a stasis field around a star and collapse it in order to make it? Maybe we could somehow get Cornish Bob's by going back in time, since we are talking miracles here."

"Well, Tracey, unless you have a time machine or another rift generator, you are not going back in time to get Cornish Bob's rift generator."

She sat quietly with a sour expression on her face, mulling this.

"So why the talk of God collapsing the wave function and making the universe?"

"Aha," he said, sipping his tea. "We progress. So if you need a miracle, who is going to do it? Will it be done with your magical powers through the force of your ego?"

"I suppose you are saying that it will be done through the power of prayer," she said flatly.

He raised an eyebrow.

"But," she said, "people pray for things all the time. They pray for winning the lottery, or for their cancer to be cured, or for their 'soulmates' to appear and whisk them off their feet. That doesn't happen."

"Right. But why not? Because there are the Ground Rules."

"That is the third time you have mentioned Ground Rules, and the Mods kept bringing them up too," she said. "So what are these Ground Rules?"

He placed his teacup gently into the saucer. "Perhaps now would be a good time to visit the Scrytorium."

He stood and gestured her towards one of the hallways leading from the main room. She rose and tentatively began walking down it towards a high, arched stone doorway some distance down the hall.

This place is certainly bigger than it looks from the outside of the building, she thought. *It must be an Otherwhen thing, like the floor between floors, or the Strawberry Garden.*

This impression was made even more obvious once she passed through the stone archway: The room beyond was very large. It was almost a sphere, with only a small, flat area on the bottom upon which sat two stone slabs, where a person could sit almost prone in a scooped-out section in the middle of each. Tracey got the impression of a planetarium where two people could recline side by side and peer into the dome above. Between the two stone chairs was a stone pedestal topped by an earthenware bowl filled with a large, glowing, green globe. The surface of the green globe morphed and shimmered, hinting at structures and patterns beneath.

Morrow took the seat on the left and indicated to Tracey that she should sit in the other. She did and discovered that the stone was not cool but warm, and she fit the contours most comfortably.

"Scrying," he began, "is the art of seeing things far away. You people have done this throughout history using crystal balls, the surface of water basins, and smoke and such. This is a little more advanced and elaborate than that."

He placed his hand on the green ball's surface, and the entire chamber leapt into light of a million stars and galaxies that filled the interior of the chamber in three dimensions.

Tracey's breath was taken away.

"It *is* a planetarium," she said, wide-eyed.

"Yes, but more," Morrow said. He slid his fingers across the surface of the green ball in a particular pattern, and a glowing triangle appeared to hover in the space above them. It flashed green and pointed downwards and to the left.

"The Scrytorium control ball reads what I intend to see and tells me what direction and magnification to move towards, and the color tells me whether to move forward or backward in time," he said, pointing to the triangle.

He traced his hand again, and the magnification increased rapidly, zooming in to show Earth floating in space.

"Your planet," he said, matter-of-factly.

He zoomed it in again, and this time it showed the interior of a jet plane, with Tracey, Ron, and several dark-suited passengers in the seats.

"Do you remember this?" Morrow asked.

Tracey scrunched her brow, thinking.

"Yes," she said. "This was when Ron and I were flying back to Seattle from the base in Denver before it was destroyed." The implications of what she was watching slowly dawned on her.

"This thing can view events from the past?" she asked, incredulous.

"Yes. Past or present. The future is dark, though, since the possibilities of things to come are just that—possibilities—

from this viewpoint, locked as we are by life in a single point of consciousness in spacetime. Once outside of that, all of this universe's path is collapsed, so the 'needle' can be dropped anywhere into the groove of the 'record,' and time can re-flow from that point. But as long as we are locked inside it, *we* can only move the 'needle' so far."

She saw Ron's mouth move as though he were speaking, but did not hear anything. She noticed that she could not hear any airplane noises, either.

"No sound?" she asked.

"No," Morrow said, with a wistful smile, "they did not see fit to give me that advantage too. I just get to read the sheet music, not listen to the song. I have learned to be pretty good at lip reading, though."

They watched the inside of the plane for a while, Tracey wondering what she was supposed to see. Tracey watched herself from the past look out of the plane's window.

"There," Morrow interjected, pointing. "Do you remember looking out of the window then?"

Tracey shook her head. Not particularly."

Morrow moved his hand across the surface of the green globe again, and the viewpoint shifted again, moving across the past Tracey's shoulder, to a view out of the window. Tracey looked again, noticed a darkening landscape, with mountains, forests, and rivers. The sun was setting on the far horizon, casting the landscape in long shadows.

"Notice anything?" he said quietly.

She shook her head. The Tracey in the picture stared absently out of the window for a time, while the landscape slowly traversed across the plane's window.

"Watch here," Morrow said. Tracey saw herself look away from the window to talk to Ron again.

"So?"

"Look out of the window," he said.

She did. The darkening landscape she had been watching dropped away, as though a chasm had opened, revealing a darker landscape beneath.

"Oh yeah, the ground I thought was the real ground was just a layer of clouds," she said. "The sun was shining on the real ground beneath."

"Yesss," Morrow said. "And look at the clouds: Do they look like real ground now?"

She scrutinized the cloud layer that she had mistaken for the real landscape. "No," she admitted. "It didn't look anything like the real ground. Why did I think it was?"

"Your mind filled in the blanks," he said.

She mulled this over.

"So, the point you are making is that I am mistaking something else for the real ground?"

She sensed, more than saw, Morrow smile.

"We are trying to discover the groundwork of reality here, which we assume to be what we know because our minds fill in that blank as well," he said.

"Like Plato's allegory of the cave?" she asked.

He considered this for a moment, then manipulated the surface of the green globe again. The viewpoint zoomed outwards until the Earth hung like a blue orb floating in space.

"If you must use a metaphor, try a soap bubble. You know, like the kind kids blow using those little wands that float around?"

"Ok, I'm picturing one," she said.

"So what makes the bubble? The soap or the empty space inside?"

"The soap," she said reflexively. "Inside is just empty space."

"True, but isn't the soap mostly empty space too? When one of those bubbles pops, what is left but a tiny speck of sticky soap? The only thing holding that whole structure together is surface tension. What do you really notice about the surface of the bubble, too? The weird colored swirling patterns, the sheen on that surface tension. Is that left after the bubble pops? So it is the invisible part holding up the visible, giving it something to form around and be held together by the surface tension. Like the view out the plane window, though, there is a real structure that is invisible underneath. Find how that works and you find out how to manipulate the bubbles from perfect spheres into other shapes. And manipulating into other shapes, of course, appears as a miracle to those who aren't doing the blowing."

"Yeah, I guess bubbles are only spheres if there isn't a wind blowing them," she said, then frowned. "So if the 'surface tension' is deformed from the perfect circle, does that mean that the bubble is more likely to pop?"

"Now you are getting it," he said.

"So we want to be the wind that deforms the shape of the universe without popping it." She thought for a minute more. "So we have the power to destroy the universe?"

He laughed softly. "Well, we can't blow that hard. We can blow our own bubbles, though."

"What do you mean?"

"Let's roll this movie back to the beginning. You know how the universe started?"

"I have been told," she said, "that there was a big bang."

"Yes. But do you know what that looked like?"

"I always envisioned some kind of fireball explosion in space...or something. Actually I have no idea what that looked like, or what exploded, or what it exploded into. Professor LaGrue tried to tell us all this stuff, but it was rather unclear."

Morrow chuckled. "LaGrue hasn't any idea what it looked like either, being focused on the surface of the windowpane. The physicists are only interested in making the math come out right to fit the theory. They are good with the 'whos,' 'whats,' 'whens' 'wheres' and 'hows' but not too keen on the 'whys.' So they can roll time back to within a tiny fraction of a second after the 'big bang' itself and explain mathematically what happened, but why did it happen at all? But before pondering that, what was there to explode and into what in the first place? It's actually an interesting question because without a framework for an 'explosion' to take place in, what could it look like? It's easy for science to explain it away by saying it is a nonsense question, but it isn't nonsense in the same way as asking what a square circle looks like, or something else impossible. We are programmed to think in this way."

"Yeah, if there was no space or time, what did the universe explode in to? And if God did it, like The Bible says, was he just floating in space as a disembodied spirit and caused the big bang?"

Morrow frowned. "What do you mean, floating in space as a disembodied spirit?"

"You know, like it says in The Bible. In Genesis."

"It wasn't like that at all. You are going to be surprised by this. Wait here," said Morrow, who shambled off and returned a few minutes later with a large, leather-bound book. He flipped through it momentarily.

Oh crap, thought Tracey. *He's pulled out a Bible.*

"Ah, right at the beginning. It says 'In the beginning God created the heavens and the earth. Now the earth was formless and empty, darkness was over the surface of the deep, and the Spirit of God was hovering over the waters. And God said, "Let there be light," and there was light. God saw that the light was good, and he separated the light from the darkness. God called the light "day," and the darkness he called "night." And there was evening, and there was morning—the first day.' It goes on to talk about the sun, moon, stars, aardvarks, and people.

"But then in John it says: 'In the beginning was the Word, and the Word was with God, and the Word was God. The same was in the beginning with God. All things were made by him; and without him was not any thing made that was made.' So which was it, Jesus or his dad?"

"Well," Tracey said tentatively, "according to Trinitarian theology, aren't they the same thing, along with the Holy Ghost?" She was uncomfortable with where the conversation was ambling. "Are you saying that they were both there floating in nothingness before space was even made, with their buddy the Holy Spirit, then God or Jesus 'created the heavens and the earth?'"

"Don't get me started," said Morrow, waving his left hand while the right manipulated the green ball once again. "I could spend hours just talking what the word 'Logos,' or 'Word,' means. If you want to see the beginning, you have to start at the beginning. Let's just watch and see," he said.

The floating Earth grew larger and larger, until it filled the entire dome before them. Tracey turned and looked behind her and saw the bright points of stars grow dimmer and dimmer as their viewpoint entered the atmosphere, until they disappeared into the blue haze of the daylight sky. She turned back and saw the ground growing larger and larger, a dusty, mostly flat landscape with a body of water or two in the distance. The ground grew bigger, like an airplane coming in for a landing, until it appeared like a view from a skyscraper.

The ground was dusty in places, with low scrubby vegetation, but there were forested patches. Even from this height, Tracey could see that an enormous construction project was under way. There were long files of workers, some dressed in loincloths, some in dingy long robes. Some were bearing stone, wood and mud, and hundreds more swarmed like ants on buildings in various states of completion.

"I thought you were going to show me the start of the universe, not the start of a town," she said.

"Ah, but we are," said Morrow. "Allow me to fill in a little back-story here. This is the city of Sepphoris. Thirty years before what we are seeing now, the Hebrews who are busy building this city revolted against their Roman overlords. The rebellion was crushed. Many were killed, many were pressed into slavery, many fled the region. But, like always, time marches on and the remaining inhabitants and some intrepid newcomers started to rebuild. The economy at this time is rather horrid. Working on rebuilding the city for the Romans is pretty much the only game in town, unless you are a fisherman or a tax collector. Lots of farmers losing their lands because they can't pay the oppressive taxes, lots of poverty, graft, corruption. Revolt is always whispered in the back alleys, but not yet openly in the streets. Soon, though!"

The view drifted ever downward from Morrow's manipulation of the green globe. They watched a narrow portion of one building being constructed now. Some workers were installing tile on a floor to portray a woman with baskets of fruit and grain. Some were building wooden forms to hold stones that were being piled by other workers into walls, while other workers smeared plaster and grout between them. Other workers carried stones, mortar, wood, water, and red roof tiles in to the other workers in baskets in long lines. The workers were wiry and dirty. One, who appeared to be an overseer, had shorter cropped hair, a cleaner tunic, and some gold jewelry. He strode about, offering direction and exhorting the workers to work faster and harder.

"So what are we looking at here?" Tracey asked.

"We are about to watch a sacking."

"A *sacking*? The universe started by someone getting fired?"

"You could say that," Morrow nodded. "It is a pretty insignificant thing to the foreman—these 'tektons' are a dime a dozen. Or a mite a dozen, you could say. But to them, it means survival or not. You see, before the Greeks and Romans conquered the land, there were lots of farms owned by individuals who did small-scale agriculture, owned what they grew, traded the surplus, and the community rumbled on. The outsiders changed things. Rome wanted taxes in coin, not barleycorn. They made it a money-based society and heavily taxed the landowners in order to pay for civic projects locally and all the way to Rome. Some could pay the tax, others could not. Those who could not had to sell their land to the city folk and lease back the land like sharecroppers. They had to pay huge rents and were able to keep just enough to survive on. Families had to have enough kids to survive childhood to work the leased land, but any extra kids and their kids had to find work elsewhere. Most of those ended up as laborers, or if they were a bit better trained, as tektons for the rich Jews who were collaborating with the Roman authorities."

"Ok," said Tracey. "Can't he get another job? Or are there are no labor unions around? I'm guessing not."

"You get the idea," said Morrow. "The tektons had to really bust their asses or they would be replaced by others who were more willing to. And if there is only one employer in town, if you lost your job you probably don't have many options. Girls would have to either beg or whore if they don't get married off, while if a young man loses his work he has only to beg. Or starve."

"So who are we looking for?"

"That one," said Morrow pointing at a young man who flashed a disarming smile while dumping a box of red roof tiles he had carried to one of the roofers.

Tracey watched him. After dropping his heavy load, he took a seat next to an old man with a long, gray beard who had likewise just emptied his box of wall rocks and appeared exhausted. Workers ambled by, leaning on shovels, and engaged in the timeless practice of "taking a breather." The young man was apparently popular.

"He has a magnetic personality, that Yeshua." said Morrow. "Of course, that tends to attract the wrong kind of attention from those in charge."

The overseer had noticed the group of lounging men and was making his way through the worksite towards them. One of the tektons saw him coming and apparently gave the warning, because the group immediately scattered, lifting shovels and mattocks and carrying baskets as they went. The old, bearded man, however, was not able to immediately stand. He tried, but sat back down, too sore or tired to scatter with the rest.

"I've had to learn to lip-read Aramaic to piece together the conversation," said Morrow. "Not an easy thing. Anyway, here is the gist of how it goes: 'All right, old timer, this is the fourth time this week I've caught you slacking off. Get out of here.' Now watch this, Yeshua hears this and comes back to help. 'Come on, Boss, give him a break. He's older than my father and still has many mouths to feed.' 'Oh, is that my problem? I have lots of men, younger and stronger, who are waiting around for a chance to work.' Ok, here is where Yeshua really blows it. "Oh, you mean your nephew?' Ha, look at that foreman's face get red. 'Ok, smartass, you know what, I actually have two nephews looking for jobs. Why don't you join the old man and get out of here too?'"

Tracey watched the foreman storm away and saw the look of anguish on the faces of the old man and the young man who had been fired trying to help him. The young man helped the old one to his feet, and together they slowly walked from the jobsite. The other workers made a point to give them a wide berth, obviously intent on not being associated with either of them. They watched in silence as the two men got farther and farther from the hive of activity, walking down the crushed limestone road to the south. After a while, the older man came to his small mud house with a thatched reed roof and tearfully embraced the younger man before entering it. The younger man, crestfallen, continued south on the road for a while, then stopped.

"Where is he going?" asked Tracey.

"His family lives in the little town to the south, Nazareth. They are poor and barely make enough for all of his younger brothers and sisters to eat, and that is with both his and his father's wages. Now with only the one of them working, there is a real possibility that some of them may slowly start down the road to starvation."

Tracey watched as the young man continued to stand there in the road, slumped in defeat. She watched his face as the thoughts churned in his mind. He stood a long time in thought, then his faced changed to a sad resignation mixed with a wistful smile of anticipation, and he struck off the road towards the Southeast.

"Where is he going? Is his family that way?" asked Tracey.

Morrow shook his head. "No, he has decided not to be a burden and doesn't want to subject either himself or them to a painful attempt to talk him out of it. He will head out into the Wilderness, looking to seek his fortune alone."

They watched him walk through the rocky, rough country for a while in silence.

"How far is he going to go? Does he find work?"

"Of a sort," Morrow chuckled. "Not what he expected, by a long shot. I'll fast-forward a bit here, as he wanders in that general direction for many days, asking to work in vineyards, as a shepherd, a fruit picker, and whatever else. No luck, though: Folks from Nazareth are known as good-for-nothing yokels. He's hearing stories of a gathering of people out in the wilderness beyond the Jordan River, of a crazy guy named John who is leading them, talking radical stuff. Turns out he recognizes the name: John is a distant cousin who he's never met."

They continued to watch, greatly sped up, as the young, now skinnier man, joined with the crowds listening to a hairy wild man as he railed at them and periodically dunked them in water.

"Wish you could tell me what he was saying," hinted Tracey.

"Maybe some other time. I'm getting to the important stuff soon. It's a lot of 'Wake up! Turn from your madness, God's holy lightning bolt of enlightenment is at hand.'"

"Wait...that sounds like it *is* the important part."

Morrow laughed. "It is! But not talking about it, or conceptualizing about it, but having it occur! Ok, I'm going to slow this down a bit. Yeshua has hung around and heard this teaching for some time now, but still hasn't found work and, in spite of getting enough to survive on because one of the tenets of the group is giving alms, he's getting weaker. I'm piecing all this together from reading lips, you know, so I'm not absolutely sure of what is going on in his head, but he's now taken off into the wilderness again and started sitting with his back against a willow tree for hours at a time. He's found the place where Elisha, one of his Hebrew ancestors, was taken to Heaven in a whirlwind. It was supposedly right at this spot, Elisha's Hill, called Hermon Hill. Yeshua has decided to wait there until God takes him up too."

Tracey watched as the sun rose and fell in accelerated time, while the young man sat with his back to the tree. She realized, after several such days, that he rarely got up, and also that she never started counting those days.

She saw a human form visit briefly, then leave.

"Wait, who was that?" she asked.

Morrow reversed the direction, then slowed it back to real time. She saw that it was John who approached Yeshua as he sat.

"What is he saying now?" Tracey asked.

"He asked if he could convince him to eat something. Yeshua said no, he was keen on getting taken up to the Father. John doesn't give up, though; he comes back a few more times. He says, 'If you are bent on doing this, why don't you just jump off a cliff?' Yeshua says, 'I don't want to put the Father to the test and force his hand.' He comes back later and says, 'Don't do this, your whole life is ahead of you, and you can accomplish anything you set your mind to,' but Yeshua says, 'Get out of here, you devil, my mind is on heaven.'"

"This is terrible," said Tracey. "How long does this go on?"

"Here, I'll slow it down now. He's been at this for forty days. Now watch carefully."

Tracey did. Morrow manipulated the green globe and the screen enlarged to a close-up of the young man's face. Tracey could tell it was slowed down to regular time. The wind gusted periodically, disturbing his long, unkempt hair. His eyes were closed, face drawn, haggard, and dusty. An insect crawled from the tree to his shoulder, then back. Another gust of wind. He continued to sit, back against the tree.

"What are we watching for?" Tracey whispered, but Morrow immediately shushed her.

Morrow panned the view back a little bit. Now they could see the ground and a bit of the tree above Yeshua's head. There was a brief flash of white light, like an old movie where the reels were being changed. When the scene resumed, Yeshua's eyes were opened and he had a slight smile. They watched for another minute as Yeshua breathed more quickly, then stood up and walked away with a purposeful stride.

"What was that?" Tracey hissed.

"That was It. The formation of the Universe. The Big Bang," said Morrow quietly.

Tracey narrowed her eyes, pursed her lips. "What? What the hell are you talking about?" she said out loud.

"That was It."

"How could that be the start of the universe? We were watching him before that flash and after. There was a universe before—we saw it."

"Yes. But it started right then, when the flash occurred. Thirteen point seven billion years before, right when that flash happened."

"I'm not following you."

Morrow rubbed his chin. "How to explain. Well, before that flash, there was *a* universe that had this young man born, raised, and working the job he recently got fired from. At the flash, the universe was born. When his eyes opened again, 13.7 billion years' worth of history was retroactively created, along with billions of years of future time. All in that flash beyond time, beyond space. It became his universe, our universe. He co-created it with God, and us. Complete with his past, his future, message, and miracles, including eventual death and rising up from that death. And we haven't even begun to ask not just how, but *why*."

"Maybe before we get to the how and why, we should stick with the *what* for a minute. What just happened?"

Morrow pursed his lips. "Have you ever seen the screen on Ron's rift generator? Oh wait, you have not seen that in this universe branch, but maybe you remember it from the other? It looks like a tree, with branches that split off with changes that are big enough to split the 'tree' into different universe lines. But those all share the same trunk, right? What our friend here just did was more drastic: He split off the other way. He in essence broke off the branch and replanted it as a new cutting. So he had a new universe line with a new trunk altogether. So he was there at the beginning, had a new history, a new present, and a new future. He blew a new bubble out of the old soap, to use the other metaphor."

"How the heck did he do that?"

"Ok, are you ready to get on to the how and why?"

Tracey suddenly felt very tired. She rubbed her face in her hands.

Morrow put his hand on her arm. "Forgive me. You are beyond tired right now, and this is a lot to take in. Let's let you finish your sleep, and we'll take this back up tomorrow."

—6—

Chris Springs, now known as Carla 23, sat at her console at the orbiting Xylol manufacturing facility and performed her job. A large, spherical bin of liquid chemical appeared from her left, attached to a conveyor chain. The chain at that point was in zero gravity, as it was in the center of the large rotating cylinder that was the factory. The chemical reaction at her part of the process required this, while later on the chain moved closer to the rim of the facility and even beyond it, where the artificial gravity was required to be stronger. The console in front of her consisted of exactly two buttons.

Chris waited until the technician inspected the chemical batch and inserted a feed tube into it. The technician gave her a hand signal, and she pressed the first button. A pre-measured portion of some kind of chemical was injected into the spherical batch bin, while the technician watched. When it finished, the technician gave her another hand signal, and she pushed the second button, sending the bin off down the chain to the next station.

Tough job, she thought.

She wondered again why this could not just be automated, like most of the rest of the facility. The reasoning escaped her, but it did provide her with the opportunity to plan the sabotage of the mind-controlling drug and the eventual destruction of the entire orbital manufacturing plant.

For the first week of her new job, Chris trained under the woman she was replacing, Kim 12. It was a challenge for Chris to remain composed, because the training consisted of being shown how to press the two buttons for hundreds of repetitions. After the first few hours of this, she was able to open a communication line to Elanor through her praying mantis familiar.

"Don't get impatient," Elanor pleaded. "I've checked her status: She has been re-assigned to the grinder."

"What do you mean, 'the grinder?'"

"You'll see," Elanor had said.

After the week of training, Chris was on her own to push the two buttons when Kim 12 retired. Around mid-shift, Elanor had called through the familiars to tell her an address to type into her computer terminal. Chris typed it in and was shown a security camera feed.

"Where did you get this?" she asked.

"I know how to poke around on the computers and keep secret about it," Elanor answered. "You have no idea what there is to see on these cameras."

Chris watched what looked like a crowded hallway in the City of God, filled with ordinary people in their papery coveralls. The crowd all seemed to be going down a certain wide hallway after being checked in by a row of people behind desks with computers. They were waiting in line, which was barely moving.

"Oh look, there is Kim 12. She's just leaving the check-in desk."

Chris watched her as she entered the line that funneled the various check in desks into the hallway.

"Ok, so what are they waiting on?" Chris asked.

"They don't know," Elanor said. "They were just told to report there now that they are retired. Other people are just stopping because they saw other people stopping and don't want to miss out on whatever it is the other people are getting. They are all getting checked in, and going down that hallway. Now watch, I'll change to another camera farther down the line...."

The view changed, the hallway was even more crowded.

"It's narrower," Chris observed. "Now there is room for only three people across."

"Right. And you can't tell by this view, but the floor is sloping downwards now a little bit."

Chris watched as they shuffled on, patiently filling the space ahead while others pushed in from behind.

"Ok, now we'll follow your predecessor even farther on."

Chris leaned forward to see that the hallway had narrowed even more, not only from the sides but from the roof as well. The people were single-file now, stooping over from the low roof, and the floor was angled down even more sharply. She saw Kim 12 stop at the back of the person in front of her, while a large man behind her blundered into her back, forcing her into the woman to her front. Even without the sound, Chris could sense the sudden jolt of alarm that the people displayed as they were herded tighter and tighter down the ever-narrowing, twisting corridor, struggling to keep their footing and avoid being crushed.

"And here is the point where it becomes the point of no return," announced Elanor.

The screen changed to another camera, which showed the corridor becoming too steep and slippery for the people to keep standing. It became a slide, one person wide. Pushed by the press of people behind, the ones in the front lost their footing no matter how much they struggled, and one by one slid off downwards into darkness. Chris watched as Kim 12 came into view, trying to hold back the tide of humanity behind her by pressing her arms into the sides of the corridor, mouth opened in a silent scream. She was not strong enough and went sliding downwards out of camera range.

"What happens to them?" Chris whispered, eyes wide.

"I told you before, when you first got here. We are here as slaves or as food. I told you she was going to the grinder. You want to see that camera?"

Chris shuddered. "No. Thank you. Let's just get on with planning this operation as soon as possible."

She pressed the second button, watched the Xylol container move down the line.

"You say you have access to the cameras. Do you know where my brother is?"

Chris heard a long pause on the other end of the familiar's arm.

"No...but I can look."

*****

After killing three of the giant scorpions with his newly assembled stinger-headed axe, the rest of them left him alone. Jeremy had assembled quite the cache of stingers, spikes, and other scorpion body part tools, and managed to hide them from the other wild people by burying them in a secret spot.

The Treehouse People cannibals proved willing to trade cordage for weapons. Jeremy did so cautiously, knowing that if they got too many of the axes they could use them on him as well, but they seemed in no hurry to risk themselves by attacking him or any living scorpions. Jeremy assumed they would use them to hunt unarmed wild men but decided that he would not worry about that. He was resolved to leave the beach area by climbing the cliff as soon as he could.

After what seemed like a month, he had assembled enough cordage and scorpion spike pitons to make his attempt. A small crowd of wild men had gathered to watch.

"You're just gonna fall and die," one of them called.

"What do you expect to find up there even if you make it? Just more monsters or worse, and no food, I bet," cat-called another.

Jeremy ignored them. He had chosen what looked like the most promising spot, where the rock face looked stable enough to support him but soft enough for him to be able to drive the shell spikes into the wall with the back of his axe.

He adjusted his paper coveralls, tied a climbing harness from a length of the rope, looped the remaining cordage across his back, and began his climb.

It was slow going. The crowd below hooted and joked about waiting for him to fall so that they could loot his weapons. After a while, one of the giant scorpions was attracted to the noise and the crowd dispersed. It took their place, waiting for him to fall. But he did not. There were many tricky places, and he was beginning to reach the end of his strength, but at length he reached the top of the cliff.

As he hauled himself over the edge, the first thing he noticed was that the terrain at the top was a vast, featureless grassland. The sun beat down on him, and he realized that he was thirsty, very thirsty. He looked back over the ledge, saw the thin strip of jungle below at the border of the vast ocean. Not a drop of it could he drink.

He adjusted his paper coveralls, now smeared with the dust and dirt of the climb, stuck his stinger axe into his climbing harness belt, and struck out into the grasslands.

After several hours, his feet were battered and seared from the flinty ground, beaten by the sun. His head ached and he was dazed. He no longer sweated.

Thankfully, the sun began to sink. He staggered on, noticing off to his left a flock of birds circling something on the ground.

Maybe a pond? He thought. Even if it was a dead animal, he might be able to sustain himself in some way.

After an hour of trudging through the darkening landscape, he saw that it was indeed a shallow, muddy lake. He ran to it with what was left of his fading strength, splashed out into it, fell to his knees and drank.

He waded back to the shore and saw that the muddy banks were covered with tracks. He examined them in the near darkness, saw that they were hooves of some sort. Exhausted, he fell asleep on the bank.

*****

Valentina Pavlov took her daughter Mandy 42's hand and together they crossed her living room and went into Mandy's bedroom, where they sat on the edge of the bed out of earshot of the prayer globe.

"How was school?" she asked quietly.

Mandy shrugged. "Same. Jimson 14 started looking at me funny when I answered a second question that the teacher asked. I had to act even dumber for a while."

"Good. Don't stand out. Be like everyone else," Valentina urged, taking her daughter's shoulders in her hands and staring intently into her clear, blue eyes, framed by the halo of pale-brown curls. She wiped the single dot of white paint from her daughter's left cheek. "We can't be caught. Eiffelia is very sneaky, and if we give ourselves away, she will make us drugged and sleepy again. You remember that?"

"It wasn't good." The girl nodded.

"That's a good girl. Now let me look at your bear."

Mandy handed over her teddy bear familiar. Valentina attached the counterfeit feed tube to the Milk intake valve, then placed the bear on Mandy's wall receptacle. The central computer sensed the ID chip of Mandy's familiar, downloaded the falsified blood test results, then dispensed Milk into the surrogate receptacle while Valentina injected saline solution into the bear's reservoir. Once the bear sensed the reservoir was full, it signaled the mainframe to stop pumping the milk. Valentina repeated the process with her own familiar, a mink. She emptied the Milk from the counterfeit feed tubes into Mandy's houseplant to defeat the sensors installed in the plumbing.

"There we go," Valentina smiled. "All done. Now Eiffelia will think we are still drugged up, as long as we keep acting like we are."

"Mommy, how long do we have to keep doing this?"

Valentina frowned. "Not much longer, honey. Mommy is working with her friends on making it so that nobody has to take the drugs anymore. But remember, even though it is bad for people, they think it is good, so we can't tell them what we are doing. Ok? This is *really important* for you to remember—right, honey?"

"Right!" Mandy clapped. "Can we watch some TV now?"

"Sure," Valentina said, leading her to the sculpted couch and activating her familiar's remote. She quickly flipped past "Super Jumbo Penises" and her own show, "Super Rape? Porn," to the latest kid's programming, "Super Anti-Demon Action Team."

Ten minutes in, right after the Team had been confronted with a phalanx of Demon Tanks, Valentina began to nod off. She was suddenly vaguely aware that there was someone standing in the shadows of her living room.

With a yelp she jumped to her feet and raised the light level with her mink familiar.

"Hello, Valentina Pavlov. Long time no see," said a voice that was oddly familiar.

She scrutinized the man standing in her living room. The body was angular, stylized, and obviously artificial. The head, in contrast, was ancient, wrinkled, gray, liver spotted—yet she recognized it.

"Professor LaGrue? Is that *you*?"

"Indeed it is," he said. "I'm surprised you recognize me."

She stood dumbstruck. "You look...different."

"Yes, my head is old because not only is it original, but I've been using it more than this timeline can account for. My body is...crafted."

She looked closer. *Did he sew his head onto a robot body?*

"Your daughter?" LaGrue asked, indicating the girl.

"Yes. Not biologically, her mother was...retired from the show."

"I see. It didn't seem to add up, time-wise. You haven't been here that long."

Valentina stood silently, not knowing what to think.

"So many questions you must have," LaGrue smiled. "Would you like to get out of here?"

"To talk?" Valentina asked. She pointed at the prayer globe in the corner. "Too late. She already knows you are here."

LaGrue shook his head. "Oh, I'm counting on that. And walking into the next room or a hallway wouldn't solve that problem, either. Eiffelia doesn't need a prayer globe to know everything that goes on in this city: Every wall and road and roof is all part of her organic cellular structure. Just like that organic spaceship hull we were studying at White Mountain. You didn't know that? No, I mean get out of here as in 'from this world.' Go home. To Earth."

Valentina's eyes grew wide. "How? How the hell can you do that?"

"The same way I got in here. I have a rift generator."

"Like the Horribles?"

"Exactly. We can talk all about it at my house. You must leave everything and come immediately."

"I'm not leaving my daughter. And there are...others who may want to come as well."

LaGrue's face soured. "Very well. Your daughter. Any others can be discussed later. But her soldiers are on the way as we speak."

Valentina grabbed Mandy by the arm and stood by LaGrue, who produced a small device from his pocket and pressed buttons.

They dematerialized with a yellow flash, and Valentina opened her eyes to find that they were on another planet. It could not have been Earth, though.

At first she thought that they had landed in the middle of a stone field, with some low hills and rock outcroppings in the distance. Then the scale of what she was looking at struck her. The rock outcroppings were columns supporting the upper reaches of a vast building. The field was actually paved stone, made with massive blocks. She turned around to look behind her and saw an oval-shaped bed, the size of a sports arena, surrounded by building-sized statues of LaGrue, in various heroic poses. Flanking each side of the gigantic bed were replicas of Egyptian Sphinxes, whose heads were replaced with LaGrue's visage. She was struck with the symbolism of his head sewed to an artificial, alien body. Mandy clung to her leg in abject terror.

She spun to look at LaGrue and found him beaming with pride.

"Welcome to my bedroom," he said, with a little arch of his eyebrows.

Overwhelmed with the ridiculous enormity and terrifying oddity of the surroundings, she burst into laughter. She did not notice the flash of shame and disappointment that crossed LaGrue's face. He recovered quickly.

"I am sure you have many questions. It has been a long time since the White Mountain days and that disastrous expedition to the Sea Tribes in the alternate universe line. Let's see...we parted when we were raided at that water treatment plant, and you were taken to Cambria to launch your...television career, correct?"

Valentina nodded and started wandering towards the edge of what looked like a cliff a few hundred yards away at the edge of the bedroom.

"And there you remained until now. Let me catch you up on the rest of the team. And this may be hard to hear. You remember Spinks was shot? Well, unfortunately, he succumbed to the wound and died shortly thereafter. Ron and Tracey were captured by Eiffelia, and Tracey was executed. Ron was kept prisoner in some universe somewhere, used for his Pangborn gene to keep it from collapsing. I have looked for him, but no luck. He could be anywhere."

"What about Smithson?" she asked, stroking Mandy's hair as she walked.

"Ah, that is the most unfortunate story of all. I know you were rather fond of him, in spite of his unfathomable blindness about it. I'm sorry to report that Eiffelia put him on an island to try to glean his knowledge for training her soldiers. She made him fight and recorded it. He lasted over a month before one of them finally got him."

She hung her head, lump in her throat, and quietly kept walking.

"My story, thankfully, was more fruitful. Eiffelia knew my value as a theorist and designer, so paired me up with my counterpart in that universe to work on her technologies. She made the mistake of assigning me to work on improving the rift generators."

As they neared the edge of the cliff, Valentina began to hear a curious murmuring sound. She could not place it in her mind.

"I told her I only needed one of the units for one day, for a mere twenty-four hours. She knew I was on the Milk, under her thrall, so she allowed it. I wanted to test its operation and decided to make a jump to whatever coordinates had last been input. Quite by accident, it just so happened that the last jump had been back to our universe. My counterpart and I made the jump, and of course I immediately reverted back to my real self, the one from our universe line. It was at that moment I realized what I had. My counterpart from that universe realized it too, of course, and attacked me! I fortunately was able to kill him."

"That is horrible," said Valentina distractedly. The murmuring noise was growing louder as they neared the cliff edge. She could not see a valley beyond the edge but could make out a mountain slope beyond where the valley must be. It was terraced with stone buildings, columns, and further terraces.

"Yes, it was dreadful. But in that moment, I realized that I had a rift generator. And knowing what it was, I knew what an immense power it was. The ability to travel to the past, or to other universes, allowed me limitless knowledge, limitless time. Do you remember back to that meeting with the Mods, back in Seattle after Cornish Bob and his goons shot the town up? Before all that babble from them about 'Cheat Codes?' You recited the words to the "Battle Hymn of the Republic" so sweetly and beautifully. Do you remember?

> *He is coming like the glory of the morning on the wave,*
> *He is Wisdom to the mighty, He is Succour to the brave,*
> *So the world shall be His footstool, and the soul of Time His slave,*
> *Our God is marching on.*

"And so it struck me, like a fateful lightning bolt, a terrible swift sword—the song was about...*me!*"

They were nearing the edge, and Valentina could just begin to see over it. The murmuring was growing louder, and it dawned on her what it was: whispering. Thousands, hundreds of thousands of whispering voices.

"Yes, Valentina. It was me who was destined to destroy Eiffelia and take her place as God. It was I who was coming like the glory of morning, it was I who was the wisdom to her might and would succor my own bravery to make myself mighty. The world would be my footstool, because I had the rift generator—

the Soul of Time—as my slave. All those years, the coded signs from the flashes of light, the birds teaching me to fly...that was what they were trying to tell me! So I went back in time, in as many universe lines as I could, and began building my power, my wealth, my influence, and my armies, with whatever intelligent races on whatever planets I could find. I knew I had the ultimate 'Cheat Code.' None of her other slaves knew what they had or how to use it. You know the first thing I did? I knew I had to give myself the idea of where to put the nuclear bomb in the trench, using the mud volcanos. I knew once they took me back to that universe, I would be traveling along a certain road in a certain car, at a certain speed, so I bought a ten-mile strip of land along that road and hired a small army of workers to install telephone poles at certain intervals, knowing that the shadows from this would communicate this coded message to myself. It was in this way that I started the war with Eiffelia! That war that she has been fighting against what she calls the monster aliens? That is *me*. Going further and further back into time to fight it. Soon, I will defeat her, and the universe will be ours."

Ours?

They reached the edge of the bedroom, and Valentina could see over the stone edge into the valley. The hillside beyond the edge was terraced with stone, terrace upon terrace dropping into the valley below. Each terrace was filled with people, a vast throng, thousands upon thousands, all wearing some kind of white toga. Valentina noted that they were not all human beings: There were oddly-shaped alien races mixed in as well. Some of the people close to the edge on the top terrace caught sight of LaGrue, and their excitement rose like a spreading wave.

LaGrue! LaGrue! they chanted. Soon, the chant spread down the valley, and before long the cry was deafening. *LaGrue! LaGRUE!*

He basked in the worship of the millions. Mandy screamed and held her fists to her ears, eyes screwed shut. Valentina lost control of her legs and slumped to the ground.

LaGrue laughed and extended his hand. "Rise, my queen! Your people have been waiting to receive you."

—7—

Without knowing exactly when it had happened, Ron and Strong realized that they had left the Dream Plains and were in some other region. The dream whirlwinds had stopped.

The dusty, brown landscape remained, but every now and then over the past day they had noticed a crumbled wall here and there, a crater, or some piece of twisted metal machinery. Off in the distance they heard what sounded like thunder, complete with flashes of light. As more time passed, they heard jet aircraft and occasional gunfire. Green and red lasers traced the sky. They stood, eyes squinting, inspecting a grayish smudge on the near horizon.

"It looks like rock," Strong said.

"Maybe. Or concrete. Not much else to do but go look."

They trudged on. The closer they approached, the clearer they could tell that it was some sort of blasted fort or battlement made of stone or concrete slabs. Ron saw something moving at the top of the structure, grabbed Strong's arm, and stopped him. Jack had stopped already. It appeared to be some kind of pole, with a protrusion at the end, and it moved around erratically. They stood watching it for a minute, unsure of what to do.

There was a whistling sound above them. From years of Ron using the sound in video war games and from Strong playing them, they both instinctively acted.

"Incoming!"

They both dove to the ground just as the shell hit somewhere behind them. The explosion was deafening, and a fine drift of dirt settled on their backs.

"Shit!" yelled Strong.

A second shell whistled by overhead. They covered their heads with their arms, and when the second impact occurred closer than the first, they were both off and running towards the tower before the last of the dust settled.

There was a dark opening between the bottom of the broken concrete slab wall and the hardscrabble dirt, and they both scrambled through it as another shell impacted the area behind them.

The fortified structure amounted to nothing more than a ring of broken concrete slabs formed into a wall, with mounds of broken rock and fill behind them forming a platform where one could stand on the battlements. A fifty-five gallon steel drum stood in the middle of the courtyard, with scraps of lumber sticking out of it. On the battlement on the far side, looking into the terrain beyond, was a man.

He was dressed in an odd assemblage of clothing, weapons, and armor. He wore what looked like a combination of football padding, chain mail, and pirate pants. His feet were clad in hiking boots wrapped around the legs with filthy linen strips and animal fur. He wore a wide leather belt, into which was stuck an assortment of knives, axes, grenades, and pistols. He wore a steel helmet on his head, painted in a crude black and white camouflage. A large, antique-looking shotgun was strapped across his back, and he was holding what looked like a jousting pike with a camera attached to the end in the air. It was this that Ron and Strong had seen waving from the wall.

"Hello!" called out Strong.

The strange man froze, dropped the pole, and extended his arms.

"Oh, you're good!" the man croaked, his voice dry as the flinty landscape. "I didn't see you coming, and I've been watching the plain for hours."

The man began crabbing sideways along the top of the wall, still extending his arms. Ron and Strong noted that where he had been standing, the stock of some kind of sniper rifle was laying on the top of the wall.

"Keep going. Slowly...," said Ron, suddenly realizing that there was a threat. He fumbled around for the space pistol that the Dwarf had given him.

The strange man turned to face them, glacially slow. He had a dusty, black beard, and some kind of goggles or binoculars over his eyes, which he slowly removed.

"*Two* of you? You couldn't have snuck up on me with two."

"No, you would have seen us if we had come from your front. We just got off the Dream Plains," explained Strong.

Another shell burst just outside the wall. Ron and Strong flinched, but the odd man stood impassively. Ron saw the gears working in the man's brain, sizing them up. He made sure the futuristic gun the dwarf had given him was aimed nearby, but not directly at, the odd man on the wall.

"Well, welcome to the War Zone." The man laughed, then snatched one of the pistols from his belt.

Ron brought his gun to bear and fired, but not before the odd man rushed a shot at them. Ron's gun unleashed a sizzling bolt of some kind of energy, which expanded as it traveled, striking the odd man's torso. With a flash of sparks, he went down screaming, a blackened mass. Ron dropped the gun in shock.

"Holy shit! I got him!" he yelled, turning to Strong.

Strong was on his knees, touching a neat hole in his chest, which began pumping bright arterial blood. He collapsed to the ground, facedown.

Ron turned him over, but it was too late to do anything. His eyes glazed over and he drooped.

Shocked, Ron grabbed up his gun and charged the wall, intent on finishing the man if he was still alive. When he reached him, he realized there was nothing else he needed to do. The man's entire body above the belt line was charred, melted. His face was mostly gone, his visage a blackened skull. He was obviously dead.

Impossibly, however, the man spoke. "Nice shot," he hissed, between skeletal teeth and jaw. "I'll get you next time."

Ron was stupefied for a full minute. "What the hell do you mean, next time?" he finally stammered. He saw that the charred corpse's jaw was starting to work, opening and closing mechanically. His fingers, no more than a blackened skeleton a moment ago, now had some kind of tarry sinew stitching itself around them.

"You know, next time. Next round," the thing hissed.

"What, you're not...*respawning*, are you?"?

"Of course I am!" the corpse hissed. "This bad, though, it might take an hour or two."?

Ron kneeled down beside the thing and disarmed it, removing each pistol, knife, axe and tossing them off the wall.

"Fucker," the corpse hissed. "Give those back."

It occurred to Ron that Strong might respawn too. He snapped his head towards him, and saw Strong sitting on the ground, rubbing his neck.

"Holy Top-Hat Wearin' Tap-Dancing Christ!" he spat, and trotted over to where Strong was sitting.

"Give me a minute," Strong said, rubbing his chest where the bullet had entered. "That *hurt*."

"*Hurt*? You were *dead*, muthafukah!"

Strong ignored him.

"Come on. We have to get back to that guy before he respawns too and tries to get even."

Strong struggled to his feet and shuffled along with Ron to the base of the wall, where they recovered the strange man's weaponry. They approached him cautiously but determined that he was not even close to being fully re-formed.

"You called this the 'War Zone,'" Ron said, crouching next to him. "What is this place?"

The charred man worked his jaw as the tarry black stuff slowly grew around it.

"You'll see. You are right on the leading edge of it now. Bad form using particle weapons against what is clearly a low-tech man."

"Bad form? You mean I broke the rules or something?" chuckled Ron.

"Well, not rules," the man croaked, his voice growing stronger. "More like Gentlemen's conventions. If you have any sport in you, you might trade up and take one of my weapons, but only if you leave one in its place. And if you want to use that ray-gun, there are parts of the storm that allow that. In these parts, it is strictly projectile and explosives only. And if you don't give my guns and blades back, I will have to start over again in the Hardcore mode, with hands and teeth only. Some might prefer that, but not me, brother."

"Look, we're new here," said Strong, his voice a bit burbly because his lung had not entirely healed. "And we won't be hanging around. But we can't have you shooting us if we give them back. We are on our way to the Gnome Sacred Mountain."

"It should be somewhere between Twentieth Century Suburbia Land and Pornlandia," added Ron.

The charred man froze for a moment, then chuckled. "Oh, right. The Storm just passed through that area. Now it is Post-Apocalyptic Suburbia and Post-Apocalyptic Pornlandia."

"What the hell are you talking about?" said Ron, feeling like he had just been punched in the gut.

The charred man's newly-forming black lips formed into a smile, and he nodded. "Yeah, the War Zone isn't fixed. It moves through Hell like a storm, and everything in its wake is ruined. Whoever is left, the survivors of whatever land the War Zone storm just passed through, now have a new story: Post-Apocalyptic versions of themselves. The old version of their book or movie re-forms somewhere else. The map of Hell is constantly shifting, you know."

"Yeah, the elf mentioned that," spat Strong. "I thought he meant that it would shift when nobody was watching whatever movie or reading whatever book was making the map the way it was."

"That happens too," croaked the man. "We get all kinds of things here."

"So if we wanted to get to that Gnome Sacred Mountain, which way?" asked Ron.

"You gonna give me my weapons back?"

"Less a few that we might need," Strong bargained.

"Fine. Not that I have much choice. But you hafta promise not to burn me again before you go. I won't come after you. Wouldn't be sporting."

"Agreed," said Ron.

The man raised a charred arm, pointed in the direction that they had been traveling."

"That way," he croaked. "Through the center of the War Storm."

*****

Jeremy thrashed awake. He was sore in every limb and disoriented. The sun was just over the horizon. He crawled through the cold mud to the edge of the pool and drank again. With a sharp intake of breath, he realized he was not alone. He scrabbled backwards to dry ground and stood, regarding the new arrival. His mind reeled to take it in, but it appeared to be a rotting corpse on a horse. It was not dead. It was dressed as a cowboy, complete with felt hat, duster, and coiled rope. His face was partially bone, the rest was rotting meat. It still had a bushy moustache. It still had both eyes, and the corpse used them as they regarded each other for some time, the cowboy chewing a stalk of grass in its lipless teeth.

"So who the hell are you, me bey?" the cowboy eventually asked.

Jeremy didn't know what to say. He pointed up, then towards the edge of the cliff some distance away.

"Oh, don't speak English?" drawled the cowboy.

Jeremy narrowed his eyes. "Oh I speak English. Wait, how the hell do *you* speak English?"

The cowboy unhurriedly regarded him, mostly skeletal hand on the saddle horn, while his horse drank. "Where you from, 'lil heller? Up there or over the cliff?"

"Both. In that order."

"Earth?"

Jeremy nodded.

"Us too," said the corpse.

"How did you get here?"

"Same as you I reckon."

"How long you been here?"

"Me? 142 years. 'Bout when she took me, they needed cattlemen too. So they buffaloed a few of these lads, got 'em drunk and dragged 'em all rufazrats through a hole in a mine into this world. Must have told the rest of the townfolk we were killed by Indians or something. Then they needed blacksmiths, tanners, butchers, whores, you name it, and started takin' them too. It was a rough town, so they probably said they were gunfightin' or who knows. Anyway, we been cattlemen for them painted-face hive people yonder across the plains ever since."

Jeremy's mind raced.

"Why aren't you dead?"

"What, never seen a zombie before? I ran afoul of the sponge, went back in time to hide from her. She found me, a'course, then took me here to keep me in eternal rotting torment by not giving me my baths often enough to keep me my byootiful self."

Jeremy did not know what to make of that, so remained silent.

"So where you from, son? Back on Earth, I mean. You American?

"Yes, sir," Jeremy said.

"Huh. Well, we best go find you a horse."

The cowboy twitched the reins, and his horse walked off towards the sunrise. Jeremy considered following him but realized he had no idea how far the cowboy was going, where the next water hole would be, or when he would get back. He trotted after him anyway.

*****

Chris pushed the first button, and the chemical injected into the spherical chamber. Technician pointed, she pushed the second button. For the twenty-seven thousandth time. Nearing madness, she opened a channel to Elanor on her praying mantis familiar.

"What have you found out about my brother?" she asked.

"Well, it's interesting," Elanor answered. "I tracked him to a particular batch of scorpion feed that I sent to the beach the same day you came, and matched his picture to the description you gave."

"Ok. And thanks for sending him off to die, by the way."

"I didn't know he was your brother. Or who you were for that matter. Anyway, I sent dragonfly drone cameras all over the area, and I was able to find three of those men still alive. Your brother wasn't one of them."

Chris was silent, clutched with dread.

"But here's the thing. The whole area down there is in uproar. Some of the food somehow managed to get themselves armed and kill some of her pet scorpions. *That* was never supposed to happen. So I saw some soldiers who had been sent in there in a shuttle to try to correct things. Soldiers and their shuttles mean cameras and records. So it seems the soldiers captured some of the food and questioned them, and they said that some new guy had killed the scorpions and, well, climbed the cliff and got away."

"Jeremy," Chris whispered.

"Maybe. Sort of matched his description, anyway. But the soldiers didn't believe them. They just confiscated the weapons and broke a few legs so they couldn't run, then left."

"So where would he have gone from there?" Chris asked impatiently.

"Up on the plateau, in the plains, I guess. Maybe got in with the cowboys."

"*Cowboys?*"

"Yeah. Eiffelia has been grabbing people from Earth for a long time. This batch got dragged through a rift a few hundred years ago for herding cattle that she uses to feed us. She also gets a lot of her best warriors from them: They send a lot of their young men who they don't otherwise have skills as conscripts to meet a quota. I dated one of them for a while."

"Well, can you send some dragonfly drones in there?"

"Maybe. They have a town near where your brother supposedly climbed up. I may have to use the drones for something else first, though."

"What?" Chris asked, irritated.

"I tried contacting Valentina 69 to ask when she would be available for our next prayer group meeting, and she didn't answer. She wasn't on her TV show, either; they were showing a rerun. Have you heard from her?"

"Why would I hear from her?"

"Well, she's missing. And her daughter is missing too."

"Did she get...arrested?"

"No, Eiffelia doesn't have her either. The records show she dispatched security people to her place, but Valentina was gone when they got there. It's like she vanished."

*****

Smithson woke in the dark on cold stone. His limbs obeyed him only slowly, indicating that he was still under the effect of some kind of drug.

LaGrue! He remembered the meeting with Ron and Strong where LaGrue had convinced Ron to hand over the rift generator, and feeling uneasy about it. After leaving, he was alone on his way back to the dojo along the gravel pathway to put the weapons away when the LaGrue twins stepped out and blocked his path. Alarm bells went off in his head when he noted that not one, but both of them held rift generators. Another pair of LaGrue twins emerged from the hedges farther down the path, and each of them also had generators. He immediately realized what was happening and turned to flee just as the third pair of LaGrues shot him in the neck from behind. The last he remembered was a dimming view of one of them putting a dart gun away.

Smithson felt the stones on the floor, found a crack. He followed the crack in the dark until his hand struck a metal bar. He found the next one, then the next. In short order he discovered that his steel-barred cell was roughly ten feet square.

The lock on the door was a pin and tumbler, but his concealed lock-pick set had been removed along with his other clothing to be replaced with paper coveralls like the Stripes wore. He sat down cross-legged on the cold stone and waited.

He did not wait long. An overhead light flickered on to reveal that the cell he was confined in was in an aircraft hangar-sized stone room. LaGrue, or what looked like him mounted on a robotic body, approached.

"Where's the rest of you?" Smithson asked.

LaGrue raised an eyebrow. "You catch on quickly. Yes, there are more than two of me now, in spite of your having grown accustomed to seeing me in a pair. He was only around because we went into the parallel universe and we met up. We went from pair, to quartet, to octet, and now we are legion. Allow me to demonstrate."

LaGrue tapped on the display of the rift generator, and then suddenly there were eight identical LaGrues standing there. "You see, all one needs to do is jump a few nanoseconds into the past, where I will still be standing before I jumped. The two of us then jump ahead and back to double us again, and again, then all eight of us return to the original coordinates, and *all eight of us have rift generators.*"

"So you figured out the cheat code," Smithson nodded. "Have you found out its weakness?"

"Weakness?" all eight of the LaGrues spat in unison. "Let us tell you of our weakness. We have been able to go back in time, amass wealth and supporters, build universe-scaled empires, and become the most rich and powerful beings in those universes. We have built fleets of starships, each powered by a duplicate rift generator and captained by one of my Others, and waged war on Eiffelia on an inter-universal scale. And you call that weakness?"

A slow smile spread across Smithson's face. "And have you beaten her?"

The LaGrues issued eight identical grunts of disgust. "No, we are thwarted at every turn, because her minions can also duplicate rift generators and go back in time in each universe to counter each of our moves. We of course go back further to counter theirs, they counter ours, ad nauseum. Thousands, maybe millions now, of universe branches where all we can do is go farther and farther back to try to destroy each other. We are deadlocked."

"Aha. So you are the alien enemy that she has been at war with all this time." Smithson paused, remembering back to the meeting at the base in Seattle where LaGrue was pondering the nature of the galactic scale wars going on, unaware that it was a future version of himself waging it. "That is what I meant by the weakness of using the rift generator cheat code like you did. You're stuck, warring with a sponge who can think independently with each cell while you try to match her duplicate you for each cell, both trying to out-jump each other in the past and destroy each other, and neither able to do anything else."

The LaGrues scowled. "Yes. But we can break the stalemate by finding more Pangborn gene carriers and keeping our universes intact while collapsing hers."

"Let me guess," Smithson said. "You want me to help you find Ron."

"Oh no, we know where he is. He's trapped in Hell like he deserved. He's just one carrier, though. We need many. We want you to help us convince the Mods to help us get out of this deadlock by giving us the Pangborn gene so we can duplicate into as many carriers as we need. They can help me defeat her."

"You've probably tried to do your little jump duplication trick while grabbing hold of a gene carrier. You've obviously discovered that this won't duplicate them too."

"Of course. It didn't work. It must be a peculiarity of the gene that it keeps the carrier from duplication. There can be only one of each carrier, no matter how many jumps or universe bubbles. I'm sure Eiffelia has tried that as well."

"So what makes you think that if the Mods somehow gave you the gene in a bottle that it wouldn't just keep you from duplicating?"

"We have to try. Experiment. Hybridize. Maybe since we weren't born with it we could still duplicate and keep the genes intact."

"And if I refuse to help you?"

"We'll kill you." The LaGrues smiled.

"Well, that won't do you any good, will it?"

"We'll just jump back in time and try again. It would be just like saving a game and repeating the scene until the speech check is passed. Eventually we'll hit on the correct wording to get you to agree, even if the chances of success for each try are one percent."

"You've already done this," Smithson realized. "How many times have you killed me?"

"You are indeed quick." The LaGrues laughed. "Does it matter? Do you want to be the next?"

Smithson felt a pang in the pit of his stomach but refused to let the LaGrues see his fear. LaGrue was right: He could have relived this scene and killed him many times. He forced himself to calmness, and to think. But the effect of eight LaGrues speaking in unison was disorienting.

"However many of me you have murdered, we must have all told you the same thing: The gene doesn't work that way. The gene was created as a sort of cheat code in itself to counteract the effect of the rift generator cheat code."

"Created? By who?"

"You could say 'the Developer.'"

"Is the Developer a Mod?"

"No. The Mods are from the same place, though. And the Mods don't work that way, either. They just don't appear when we snap our fingers or call. They initiate the contacts."

"Yes, so you have said. But from where?"

Smithson blinked.

"Look, Smithson, I know you have some kind of 'relationship' set up with these Mods creatures. Some kind of super-secret club of inside cool-kids with little tridents. And I know you have mentioned some kind of training program, and you have started Tracey on this."

"And?"

"And so we want you to tell us what you know about them so we can use a rift generator to go to wherever they are and negotiate with them."

"They aren't anywhere your rift generator can take you to."

"Why not? They are capable of taking us to any point on any branch that ever was."

"Have you been able to jump to one of those 'Otherwhen' sites? Like the floor between floors at the office building in Seattle?"

The LaGrues looked puzzled, then one of them manipulated his rift generator and vanished. He reappeared moments later.

"No," that LaGrue reported. "I was able to walk into the building and the elevator but could not jump to it from either place."

Smithson waited while the LaGrues walked away to discuss the ramifications of this. They approached him after they finished.

"Explain," one of them demanded.

"Look, LaGrue, I'm really sorry. You have grandly and intricately messed up your entire life. I'm not sure you can fix this short of just throwing in the towel."

"Explain."

Smithson exhaled with exasperation. "You have already had it all explained. The Mods told you what it was all about way back there in Seattle. You just didn't accept it because you labeled it as 'supernatural.' It is, in the sense that it is a truth beyond the natural laws as they exist in this time-space continuum."

"There is nothing beyond this time-space continuum, by logical definition," said a LaGrue.

"Spoken as a true character in a movie who doesn't realize that someone is holding the DVD he is on right before they put it back in the movie player and run the thing. Or a fighter-mage character in a Dungeon Throne game who doesn't realize that he is really a twenty-something kid playing online with his friends."

"That is an unacceptable explanation. If someone is holding a DVD, or a game controller for that matter, they are themselves in a universe line, and unless there is some inherent limitation in the rift generator, that universe can be accessed like any other. I can only deduce that the rift generators are inherently flawed by design since they cannot access the 'Otherwhen' line."

"Otherwhen isn't a universe line like the one we are in now. Or like Hell, for that matter. It isn't a branch or the trunk. It is the ground where the tree grows. It isn't a bubble but instead the ocean it is suspended in. But beyond both, metaphorically speaking, is the sky. And that is where the Mods are."

Smithson watched carefully while the LaGrues calculated this data.

"We are going to need further explanation," one of them said. If the Pangborn Gene was inserted by the Developer to counter the 'cheat code' of the rift generator, how did the rift generator enter the universe to begin with? Did the 'Developer' err in his design?"

Smithson considered his answer. *If I tell them the truth, will they change course and solve this thing? They are intelligent enough to grasp the implications and are breaking the ground rules already. And if I don't, I might end up dead and have to make this decision again when he 'reloads' this scene.*

"Ok, LaGrue, I'll tell you the history here, but I doubt you'll believe it. It is admittedly pretty fantastic. How to begin? Have you ever wondered why almost every culture on Earth has mythology that is remarkably consistent on many fronts? How they have magic, wizards, witches, dragons, elves, trolls, all that stuff? Well, that's because once upon a time, long ago, that was real."

The LaGrues regarded him quietly, each with one eyebrow raised.

"I told you this was hard to swallow. Anyway, back when the world was young and players first entered this great Massive Multiplayer Game from beyond, the rules were more fluid. The Developer and Players were co-creating as they still do, but they were loosey-goosey and played with...well, played *as* dragons and wizards and inter-dimensional tinker elves and golems and animated armor suits and talking animals and you name it. The good Players got better and better at utilizing magic. They 'leveled up,' you might say, and became incredibly powerful and immortal, while the less-skilled players had a harder go of things, and life for them got a bit more dreadful over time. You know, cannon fodder and serfs serving omnipotent dark lord masters and all that. For a long time, they lived with that as good story elements. Eventually it got worse, so they petitioned the Developer for relief. He sent The One to save them from the evil master. You know how that myth went. Hooray, the world was saved! Well, eventually another evil master dark lord of dread power arose, and another hero was sent. This one became the next dark overlord. The cycle repeated and repeated. The minions petitioned again, saying, 'Hey this game is getting less and less fun,' so eventually the Developer called a big meeting to settle the problem. Call it 'The Council of Eden' or something. The Developer said this kind of gameplay was not in the original design. It wasn't structured enough to make a good storyline, so the fun and learning were limited because they weren't balanced as he originally designed. Half of the players wanted to continue playing no-holds-barred crazy, saying the fun outweighed the learning. The other half also disagreed with the Developer and said the learning should outweigh the fun. The Developer said, 'Ok, as you wish,' and then made a separate universe branch that would run alongside the main one, where the players called the shots and did most of the creating. Players who wanted to do that style could go there, and those who wanted the more arduous path would stay in this world, now bereft of magic by way of mutually agreed-upon ground rules. These ground rules meant no more magic. And not only that, but the memory of how things were, with the magic and super powers, would be relegated to myth and legend only. 'What if we change our mind and want to go to the no-rules zone?' asked the Stayers. 'I'll leave rifts, holes to the other world,' said the Developer. 'You will retain myths of that other world, called Faerie, or Hell, or Valhalla, or whatever, to be available in various places that are difficult to find but findable to those who really want to get to the other side.' 'What if *we* change our minds and want to play hardcore mundane?' asked the Goers. 'Well, we can't have you coming back and remembering how to do magic—that would defeat the purpose,' said the Developer. 'So I will leave a rift generator in the hands of a special band of created beings in your world, so if you want to return you can do so in such a way that would erase the version of you that has those memories.' So he created the rift generator and recruited the lawn gnomes to guard it in their sacred mountain, tasking them to return players who changed their minds to the regular world by way of leaving them as amnesiacs or infants under cabbage leaves and such. So that is how it went. For a while. Because there's always one bad apple. One of the players, over in Hell, decided she knew better and wanted to control the mundane world, like the good ol' days. She whispered lies and deceits into the ears of one of the sacred gnomes and convinced him to plant her with her knowledge intact in the mundane universe long, long ago in history as a sponge. She grew powerful over the eons, even without the active magic, and the gnome with his stolen rift generator became her first servant. He couldn't hang around to face the wrath of the other gnomes, of course. They've been seething about it and wanting their rift generator back ever since. Once the Developer started losing a few universe lines, he had to inject the Pangborn gene as a line of code to keep them from collapsing. Eiffelia has been hunting down and killing the carriers that she couldn't convert ever since. So here we are today."

The LaGrues stared at him a long while. "That is the most preposterous thing I have ever heard," they said in disturbing unison.

Smithson shrugged. "Told you. Have you seen the twin branch on the rift generator screen like Ron did? Have you ever sent over any of your duplicates to see what it was?"

"We tried, but the rift generator would not allow the jump."

"Did you wonder why? It's because you are not a gene carrier. The rift generator was designed to go one way unless you are a lawn gnome or Pangborn carrier. But if you want some verification, how about you jump back in time to the universe before Hell was split off? See for yourself. Yourselves."

The LaGrues narrowed their eyes and in unison lifted their rift generators. They scrolled far, far down the screen. As one, they all vanished.

Smithson waited, and before long they returned, looking haggard and shocked. One of them approached Smithson's cage closely.

"I must find a way to incorporate that power into the present universe. Then I will be able to beat her."

"That won't work, by design. Otherwise she would have done it long ago."

LaGrue pondered this. He nodded.

"I have made a grave mistake," the LaGrue announced. "There is no way out of this loop. However many duplicates I make of myself, each going back in time to cut off and eliminate one of Eiffelia's rift generators, she utilizes the same tactic against mine. I had hoped the stalemate could be broken by utilizing the Pangborn gene in a way that Eiffelia has failed. I was in error. The Mods explained this, but I could not accept their premise. Your story is even more preposterous. Still, the evidence is strong and consistent with your explanations." He paused. "There is only one way out of this situation. Existence itself is at stake."

A sense of dread quickly enveloped Smithson when he noted the LaGrues started stealing clandestine glances at each other. Having learned through training over his lifetime to trust his instincts, he dropped prone onto the stone floor an instant before the eight LaGrues blossomed into a multitude, who simultaneously drew guns and began shooting each other.

—8—

Tracey regarded Morrow with narrowed eyes. "That is the most preposterous thing I have ever heard."

Morrow shrugged. "Told you. I know it's hard to believe, but there it is. I agreed that you have reached the point in your training where, without this knowledge, further progression would be meaningless. Remember I warned you that if I told you this, and you believed it, you would be at risk for losing your zest for this life. This is the dusk before the proverbial dark night of the soul. You must keep faith that you will come out the other side and want to live again."

Tracey placed her fists at her temples and exhaled sharply. "What do you mean 'if I believe it?' And even if I did, why would I lose my interest in living?"

"You can always believe something but refuse to grasp the enormity of it. Or you can simply choose not to believe something. Even if you see it."

"Where would I see this aside from you just telling me?"

Morrow glanced over his shoulder down the hallway and resumed regarding her with a half-smile.

"Ah. The Scrytorium. Well let's go see." Tracey scowled and started down the hall, resisting the urge to either stop or run.

She settled into the stone seat. For the past six weeks, she had grown adept at using the artifact, silently observing all manner of historical events and learning many facts that were lost or obfuscated to the known canon of history. Aside from this, however, Morrow had done little by way of instruction. He seemed content to putter about, sipping tea and enjoying meals and music, while she explored.

"Ok, so where do we go? I've gone all the way back to the dinosaurs and have yet to see the first dragon, troll or wizard flying his castle through the sky."

"Have you discovered the alternate universe/timeline feature?" he asked.

"Uh, no," she answered surprised. It had not occurred to her to wonder about this.

"So roll us back to our friend under the willow tree on Elisha's Hill," instructed Morrow. "Good. Now expand out so we see the whole planet. That gives us a view of the whole world at that moment in time."

They watched the Earth suspended against the starry background for a moment.

"Ok, now what?"

"So now double-tap the green globe to get us into alternate mode. This replicates the screen on a rift generator that shows the alternate universe lines, but on a larger scale."

Tracey rapped the globe with her palm, and immediately an overlay of two ghostly glowing tubes appeared, passing parallel through the globe, one orange and the other blue.

"So what are those?"

"The blue channel," answered Morrow, pointing, "is our current state of affairs. Our history line without weirdness: the hardcore reality players. The orange channel is the one which has the free-form players, the superheroes, wizards and mythic beings. This is the moment when they diverge, when Jeshua had his flash and created them both retroactively. Try moving back in time right before he did that."

Tracey rolled the timeline back a short distance, and the blue line disappeared.

"That is what would have happened if he had not had his Moment. There was only the weird line. If you dialed back to observing history mode in that orange line, you would see that the history you looked at earlier would be quite different. Instead of being a Tekton building a villa, Jeshua was a powerful wizard, working miracles. He sat under the willow tree because he was bored with the way the game was being played and wanted the game to be played with fewer lightning bolts and more love and honesty driving the storyline. Others were dissatisfied too and wanted to scrap the program and start a different 'game' with more mundane rules. Instead, he chose to recreate the world from the beginning with both types of players getting what they wanted. He started the blue line all the way back. Now, from that moment on, there was one straightforward history with the laws of science controlling, and another history with the laws of magic and will-directed reality. One line evolved dinosaurs over millions of years; the other bred dragons with the wave of a wand. For the hardcore players, who didn't want the cheat codes, suddenly things had always been that way and the inhabitants didn't know any different. The lovers of more free-form play continued on their orange line as though nothing had ever happened. Now, instead of being tempted by the Devil to change things back to the way they were after he made the great divide, there was John checking on him under the tree, like you saw in our history."

"And Jeshua?"

"Ah, since he was the new co-programmer, he walked in both lines. He shared our history but had enough of the old line that he could be born of a virgin, walk on water, calm storms, heal the sick, raise the dead. It worked almost flawlessly. There were a few cheaters who remained in the blue line just to mess things up. There was this one guy named Simon Magus who did that, but they convinced him to go while he was flying around Rome. But they were nothing next to the big cheater."

Tracey mulled this silently for some time. She stood and wandered back to the main room, with Morrow trailing leisurely behind. She helped herself to some tea, which had grown cold. She drank it distractedly anyway.

Thoughts chased each other through her mind. She thought about their series of blue universe lines and the corresponding orange/hell line. She thought about the Pangborn gene. Rift generators. Eiffelia.

"So Eiffelia is the big cheater who convinced one of the gnomes to insert her back into the blue line. But she wasn't a programmer herself. Why didn't she stay in the orange line and be able to use any powers and magical skills she wanted?"

Morrow rubbed his chin and exhaled. "We have been trying to understand her motivations for a long time. We thought at first that she was flawed or diseased. Over time we realized that she was just plain evil. Her ego drives her. Power over others feeds her ego. Little egos have the unholy craving to be the biggest, most powerful. Fear feeds her power, fear of others becoming more powerful and limiting her ego by comparison. She specifically planned her insertion into our universe, remember. There, in hell, she was a mediocre talent. There, the more skillful players kept leveling up and increasing their powers until they were god-like, and struggled with each other for dominance with thunderclouds and black hole bolts. None of them could harm the others, and dominating the weaker players grew boring. Eiffelia was not as skilled as those, and could not contend with them. When she turned her wrath on the weak, the ones stronger than her slapped her down. So she planned her escape into the blue line. Not by the way it is allowed, by being re-inserted without memory as a foundling or an amnesiac, but by coming intact as a sponge."

"Why a sponge?"

"Hearken back to your time as a marine scientist. Sponges are a loose collection of individualized cells, not tissues. They are like holograms. Any one cell can grow back the entire animal. She didn't want to come to the hard-core blue line universe only to die like all the rest of the players, even with the power of the cheat code rift generator. She wanted to grow for millions of years to the point that she could be immortal in this world like she would have been there."

"They are immortal there?" Tracey asked.

"Ah," Morrow smiled. "I forgot to mention that in Hell one cannot be killed by others. That is pretty much their only 'ground rule.' If you are destroyed by another dweller of the hell line, you 'respawn' and keep playing."

"Forever? How horrible."

"Your realization of this gives me hope for you. Yes, they keep respawning, but they are not actually trapped forever. They can quit the game themselves and return to the same place we end up when we leave our version of the game. But they only get to do it once."

"Wait, we get to do...what...more than once? I'm confused."

Morrow stood, paced the room while searching for words. The monkey man brought him some fresh tea, which he poured for them both.

"I told you earlier that I thought you were ready for this. I hope I am right. Are you ready to proceed?"

She raised an eyebrow, nodded.

"Have you ever played an open-world video game?" he asked.

"No, but I have seen Ron play them. And play them. And play them."

"Do you know the basic mechanics, though? You fire up the TV, turn on the game console, navigate to the game you have saved, then the machine loads the saved game and away you go. You are playing as a character in a fantasy world. Right?"

"I'm with you so far."

"So who are 'you' at that point? Are you the player manipulating the game controller, or are you the character on the tv screen? Who is the 'first person' in a first-person game?"

"I am always the player with the controller, but I'm experiencing the game through the character and his or her persona."

"Right you are. Just so." Morrow paused again, seeming to wonder down what path to proceed. "So you're playing along and you have to quit and go make a sandwich or mow the lawn or something. What do you do?"

"I think you save the game and it freezes that world, and you get on with your life."

"Exactly. So what happens to the character in that game while you are eating your sandwich?"

"Nothing, I guess. Time is frozen until the saved game is loaded back up."

"Yes, if it is a single-player game. Even if the time it takes you to get back to the game is an hour or a week or a year. The real life continues at its pace; the game life is on an entirely different plane. But if it is a multiplayer game, the time continues for the other players while your character just vanishes or sleeps for a while."

Tracey nodded. "Ok, so if our life here, what we consider the 'real life,' is by analogy just the video game and we have a 'real life' beyond what we understand, then are you saying that we have pauses where we are doing things in our 'real life' that we don't experience here?"

"There are some we don't experience. But if you think about it a minute, we also have breaks in the story that are built in." He paused for Tracey to catch up.

"Like...unconsciousness?"

"Yes, in a way. But not necessarily as dramatic as getting knocked out with a right hook or getting anesthetized for tonsil surgery. We go unconscious most every night."

"Oh, sleep of course."

"We're getting there," Morrow said. "But sleep is a funny thing. Sometimes we lay our heads on the pillow and we wake up the next morning like no time at all has passed. Other times we dream. Sometimes the dreams seem to take only minutes, sometimes they feel like years are going by."

"So I assume that the one where no time passes corresponds to the player saving the game and then mowing the lawn or eating a sandwich or something. What is going on with the dream?"

"That is kind of like when the player goes to make the sandwich but leaves the game going."

Tracey thought about that. "So part of us stays in the game?"

"Part of us never leaves the game. And how much stays depends."

"On what?"

Morrow smiled and raised his eyebrows, signaling Tracey that she was to reason this out.

"Ohhh-kay," she sighed. "So on one extreme, we save the game and wake up in the morning and don't remember anything. On the other extreme, we have vivid dreams and wake up and remember all of them."

"Almost correct. On one extreme we wake up and remember nothing, but the other extreme is only applicable for normal people. Those who have the recessive Pangborn Gene have a more...extreme extreme."

Tracey blinked. "What do you mean?"

"Well," said Morrow, "sometimes they go to sleep still playing the game. The dreaming becomes the new gameplay."

"I'm not following you."

"Tracey, do you remember when you first came here?"

"Sure. I followed the flying pickle here and cut up my feet and argued with the lady in the Chinese restaurant downstairs."

"Right. But before that?"

Tracey squinted, searching her memory. *Maurice told me I would dream and it would take me to Andrew Morrow. I went to sleep, then opened my eyes and saw the flying pickle in my room....*

With a sudden landslide of realization, she knew that she had not woken up when this happened. She was dreaming. She had been doing so for weeks. She was still sleeping in her bed.

"I gotta wake up, " she growled. Her vision darkened around the edges, and she felt her feet under the sheets.

She felt a sudden shock of warm liquid in her face, and Morrow grabbed her by the arm and started walking her around the room. He started singing in a strong voice.

"Großes, das ins Herz gedrungen, blüht dann neu und schön empor..."

Tracey wiped her face. Morrow had spashed her with his tea, and it was sticky with sugar.

"Hat ein Geist sich aufgeschwungen, halt ihm stets ein Geisterchor...."

"What the hell are you singing? Is that German?"

"Nehmt denn hin, ihr schönen Seelen, froh die Gaben schöner Kunst..."

"I get it. You needed to get me back here and grounded in this...dream? Reality?"

"Wenn sich Lieb und Kraft vermählen, lohnt den Menschen Göttergunst."

"Come on Morrow, help me out here."

"Sorry, just wanted to finish the stanza. The Fantasy in C Minor is one of my favorites. I thought I had lost you for a second there! So here you are in the midst of your own miracle, like we asked for when you first got here."

"So I'm sleeping in my house and this is all a dream."

"It could be that way," he said, watching her carefully. "But if you think of it as the 'real' you sleeping back in your house and this being 'just a dream' you, then the miracle hasn't happened yet, and you will have failed when you 'wake up' back there. None of this will have happened. The *real* 'real' you is here. In the flesh and blood. Waking and sleeping, and experiencing and learning. The new universally-shared reality with all the other sentient beings who share this game."

"So where is my body that fell asleep and is having this dream? I am still back there in my bed, right?"

"Nope. You are you, right here."

"But I have a physical body back there too. Am I a new duplicate?"

"You only have a body there if you choose to wake up there instead of here. Think of it like an old saved game that you can load back up. You can keep playing this saved game version the rest of the way. You are physically here, more so than there. And at the risk of really scrambling your eggs, this is not the first time you have done this. Just the first time you have done it intentionally. Your recessive gene, in a way, is just as powerful if not more so than the full gene like Ron has. He can keep universes from collapsing, but you can change them from the inside through dreaming."

"So I can dream of flying and shooting lightning bolts from my fingers and have it really happen?"

"No. There are still the Ground Rules. You could do that stuff if you were in the Orange Line, but not in our reality. If other co-creators saw that, the Blue Line covenant would be invoked and the game would reboot at a point before you pulled magic off. That is why you just can't dream Eiffelia out of existence. But you *can* do things that aren't impossible. Miracles can happen to you if they are possible. Hence I am a human being, and Smithson is a martial arts expert. He didn't always have that past, you know. He retroactively created that. He just woke up one morning and had a past where he was a SEAL and learned to be a ninja."

"So I can make a past where I was a concert pianist or a master assassin or something, because that is *possible*. But I can't be Supergirl because it's impossible."

Morrow nodded.

"But you said when I got here that getting Ron out of Hell was impossible."

"It's not that kind of impossible. I said it would take a miracle."

Tracey took a deep breath and narrowed her eyes, thinking for a long time.

"So what do I need to dream?"

Morrow smiled, nodded. "Now we're talking. Good work."

—9—

Ron squinted into the digital binoculars at the Sacred Gnome Mountain's fortifications through the arrow slit in the stone walls a mile beyond the Gnome border. The assault of the prior day had breached the castle walls after crossing the poison and lava moats but had been repulsed by the lightning drones. Their own walls had been hastily raised in defense against the Gnome bombardments of molten lead shot, plasma cluster bombs, and tungsten flechettes,

"What are the little bastards doing?" asked Strong.

Ron shook his head. "Can't see. They're pretty small, and the trolls they have defending are well camouflaged. Have the Saxons and Space Marines finished respawning?"

Strong grunted. "Yeah, the ones whose bodies we could recover. Who knows what the Gnomes are doing with the rest. I still think we are wasting our time. But if you insisted on trying, we should have recruited better back at the War Zone. If you had been willing to tell them that this was to recover the rift generator ball, we might have talked Superman or Thor or those wizards from—what did they call it? Propilandria or something?—into coming."

"I still disagree, Strong. If some superhero or powerful group gets its hands on a rift generator, what would stop them from keeping it instead of giving it back to us?"

"Hmm. The ones we got may be worse, though—they just came along for the mayhem."

A Viking and a seven-foot-tall Bigfoot creature approached them, climbing up the small hill to the concrete bunker where they stood, dodging from cover to cover behind shattered stone walls and craters. Ron and Strong remembered the odor this time and surreptitiously affixed water-soaked bandanas across their faces as the two approached.

"Hail Golden and Strong!" the Bigfoot said with an oddly unfitting high-pitched, melodious voice.

"Yes, uh, greetings!" said Ron. "What tidings?"

"We have devised a plan to neutralize the lightning drones by placing a dark energy and necrotic mana-charged arcing Tesla field generator near them," said the Bigfoot. "The pulse will travel along their control and navigation energy field and jump from unit to unit. It should take them all out in one stroke."

"We just need to get it close enough without getting killed," said the Viking.

"Let's send in a shapeshifter," said Strong. "He can creep in looking like a blowing piece of debris or something."

"Yeah. Blow in some other debris as extra cover," said Ron. "Whatever can cross the trenches without getting stuck."

"And once the lightning drones are down, will you authorize an all-out assault this time?" urged the Viking.

Ron nodded. "Why not. Let's send the lot this time; they can always respawn if they run into some new, sneaky defense. Just make sure we recover as many bodies as we can this time. Coordinate with the orbital bombardment from the dreadnought class star cruisers and air cover from the Spitfires and levitating laser cannon platforms. Might as well throw in the flying monkeys with paralysis wands. And a phalanx of war cats with Splatter Casters."

"No Splatter Casters," warned the Bigfoot. "They will hinder the Phoenician Venom-Slingers."

"Very well," Ron sighed. "Then use Gush Clusters. And maybe an Ouroboros Mine. We attack at dawn."

The Viking leered his approval and strode off to arrange the offensive.

Strong exhaled sharply and turned away.

"You don't think this is going to work, do you?" asked Ron.

"No. Look, there are still...*things* that I have not talked about from that time I got fried and respawned myself. I told you when you were recruiting soldiers for this campaign to recover your rift generator that it wouldn't work. I'm telling you again you are wasting your time."

"Right. And are you going to tell me this time why that is?"

"I told you, I can't. That was part of the deal."

"What deal?"

"Again, can't say."

Ron threw up his hands in frustration.

"Look, your cryptic commentary is not helping. I have to get that rift generator back to get out of this hell and to get Tracey's kids out of theirs. So either help me, tell my why you can't, or get out of the way."

"I said I would help, and I am helping. I'm just also saying that you are wasting your time."

"The only time I'm wasting is talking to you, apparently. You know what? Maybe I should just get myself killed too so I can respawn with this super-secret squirrel knowledge that you have."

"No. Don't do that, buddy. Bad mistake."

"Yeah? Why?"

"You wouldn't be able to leave."

Ron opened and closed his mouth, stunned. "Wait, what? What do you mean? If you die and respawn here you can't leave? Does that mean you can't leave here?"

"That was part of the deal. Well, it's part of the deal for everyone here. But I can't disclose that."

Ron sat down against the stone wall and held his head in his hands.

"You can't leave? You're stuck here?"

"Yeah. But frankly I probably would have chosen to stay here whether I had gotten killed or not."

Ron shook his head incredulously. "How can you say that? Your life is back in the real world."

Strong considered his response carefully. "This is the real world too. Look, I can tell you this much. It is going to sound really crazy, though. I know it did when they told me."

Ron waited.

"Ok, you remember what the Elf and Dwarf said to us earlier about this being a world made by humans? Well it is now, but it was not always that way. A long time ago, our universe and this one were intertwined. Back then, we were able to do all the stuff we can do here. Superpowers, magic, the full meal deal. But remember how this is all just a big MMORPG? Well some of the 'players' wanted to play in hardcore mode, without all the powers and magic and other cheat code stuff. They thought it was getting out of hand and were bored with the lack of challenging game play. The players here disagreed and said that the vanilla mode would be the boring play. So the big 'dungeon master' in the sky split it into two games: one hardcore vanilla and the other this one."

Ron considered this for a long time.

"That is the most preposterous thing I have ever heard."

"That's what I said, brother!"

"So what does this have to do with my rift generator?"

"That was originally an escape point from here back to our world, left in the hands of the Gnomes to administer. Eiffelia corrupted one of the Gnomes to steal it and bring her back into our universe line with her knowledge intact. She started using it to manipulate universe lines and the 'Big Programmer' made us Pangborn carriers as a de-bug code. The Gnomes have been itching to get their rift generator back for a long, long time. We were the first ones stupid enough to use it to come back here, and the Gnomes were waiting for it. So that's why I think you are wasting your time trying to get it back."

"You're right. That *is* the most preposterous thing I have ever heard."

"Told you."

"But wait, if all this is true, what deal did you make and with who?"

"With the ones in the real world. Where us players come from."

Ron squinted, confused.

"Look, when people in our world die, they have ended that life game. They go back to the reality that exists beyond time, space, and dimension. The world beyond. Then they can either stay there and live whatever it is they live, or play another game. They can live another life game, with no memory of the last game, either in our universe or starting another game here in Hell. If someone who has started a game here dies, they respawn pretty much indefinitely, at least until they want to quit. Permanent death has to be self-inflicted. So when I, as a product of our universe, died here in this one, it put them in a quandary. They had to either adhere to our ground rules and have my game ended, or adhere to the rules here and have me respawn. We worked it out: I would respawn but could not talk to you about anything beyond what you would know. And to hold me to that, they removed any memory of what that was, other than the bare facts about it. So here we are."

Ron stared at Strong like he had just admitted he was a ghost.

"So...hmm. Ok. So how do I ever leave here? How do I get Tracey's kids?"

Strong shrugged.

Ron frowned, stood, and paced the stone room.

"There is only one thing to do," he said, and walked with determination out of the room.

Strong followed, curious. Ron made his way down from the battlement, found the gate, and ordered it opened. He left the fortification and strode boldly towards the Gnome mountain lines.

"Uh, buddy, they have live ammo!" warned Strong.

Ron paused, cast about, and observed a detachment of his Dacian warriors guarding some fallen Crusaders as they respawned. He tore the white robe off of one of them and continued his path towards the mountain, waving the white flag over his head.

They crossed their front lines, bristling with weapon barrels, rocket nose cones, and sensors of every description. The no man's land was pockmarked with craters and charred ash for a mile, and they crossed it with trepidation. The landscape beyond was bare and rocky, gradually sloping upwards to the heights of the Sacred Gnome Mountain. They continued, half expecting at any moment to be blasted into oblivion.

"Halt," grated a voice so deep it seemed to come from the earth itself.

Ron and Strong stopped.

"Scan them," said another gravelly voice. They were enveloped briefly by a barely visible white haze.

"Unarmed and free of spy devices," said a third.

A large rocky section of the hillside detached itself from the ground and formed into a roughly humanoid shape.

"Troll," whispered Strong.

"What business have you on Sacred Gnome Mountain?" it asked.

"I seek a parlay with the Gnomes," answered Ron with the slightest quaver in his voice.

"Wait," the troll rumbled.

They waited. After a while they saw a tiny red hat bobbing down the mountain. The animated lawn Gnome stopped ten yards uphill, arms akimbo. He scrutinized them carefully for a full minute.

"What do you want?" he asked, munching his beard.

"I want my rift generator back," Ron answered.

The Gnome barked out a laugh. "You mean *our* sacred treasure. The one that was stolen from us in past ages that you graciously and stupidly returned."

"It wasn't me who stole it. I need it back so I can get out of here and get my stepkids back from Eiffelia."

"Not our problem," smiled the Gnome. "So I guess you can get back to wasting your time attacking us. Bigger, better armed, and more imaginatively commanded armies have tried taking the treasure from us before, and they have all failed. You too will fail. This has been mandated from on high."

Ron did not know what to say. His face fell.

"Look, here's what I can do. Now that we have the treasure back, we can get working on the many hundreds of years' worth of backlog of getting people out of here to go live in your world. We haven't been able to do our job without our God-given treasure. I'll run you right to the front of the line and send you back to your world with a new body and no memory. You can choose grown amnesiac or infant. Infant is the way to go, in my opinion: You get a whole lifetime instead of a partial. Especially useful for an old schmuck like you. Used to be in the old days we would leave 'em under cabbages in the garden, but now your world would find that surprising. I guess we will just start populating orphanages."

"No, I need to get back to my world as me."

"No dice. Our Sacred Task using our Sacred Treasure from our Sacred Mountain is quite specific. Nobody leaving here can do so with memory of what this realm is about."

"Ah, but I haven't learned any wizardry or gotten any superpowers. Scout's honor!"

"Not that you know of, human. But the denizens of this place have weird ways of permeating you. One can catch these things like viruses. No, it's our way or none. Why so stuck on going back as you anyway? Is your ego so special to you? Just start a new game as a new character."

Ron examined the diminutive Gnome closely. He detected no trace of pity or flexibility in the small, bearded face. The Gnome was a force of nature.

"No thanks. I'll be back if I ever change my mind."

Ron turned and walked slump-shouldered back towards his battle lines. Strong wrapped an arm around him.

"So, what do you wanna do now, buddy? Should we go to Middle-earth? Arrakis? Ringworld? Tatooine? Maybe we should learn some wizarding first—"

"Give me a damn minute, Strong, will you?"

Ron puzzled all the way back through the troll-occupied no man's land.

"I have it. The way out!"

"Do tell," said Strong, surprised and somewhat disappointed.

"The dream plains! We go back there and find Tracey while she's having a dream. She dreams a lot, you know."

"Well, that sounds like the longest of all long-shots in the history of all long-shottery. You know there are millions and millions of people who 'dream a lot.' And besides, in the entirely unlikely event you happen to stick your head into a dream whirlwind and find it to be Tracey, what then? What is she going to do?"

"She's going to build a new rift generator. Back when I was trapped in Eiffelia's base at the bottom of the ocean, I got a visit from Pops's ghost. He told me that the papers he was working on were plans for making a rift generator. Those plans are still in my old house where I was starting to clear his stuff up but was procrastinating. All Tracey has to do is go home and follow those diagrams."

Strong raised his eyebrows in surprise.

"You got a visit from a ghost?"

"I know it sounds crazy. But is it any less crazy sounding than blowing this off and riding a magic carpet to Earthsea to learn wizardry?"

"You have a point."

"So now we just have to find Tracey in one of her dreams and tell her where the blueprints are."

"Hold your ponies, my optimistic friend. It will be one thing to build the generator, but where are you going to get the golden orb to power it? You plan on surrounding a star with a gold shell and collapsing it with a stasis field to the size of a marble?"

"Why not? Hell has all kinds of advanced space-faring civilizations here. All we gotta do is find one and get them to build us a gold marble."

"Then why didn't the gnomes just do that? Why did they need *our* gold marble from the rift generator? I'll tell you why, compadre: It's because the part that you can build using your Pappy's plans isn't the hard part."

Ron's shoulders sagged.

"It's ok, buddy," said Strong, patting Ron on the back. "It isn't so bad. You wanna go drink something blue at the Creature Cantina?"

"No, thanks. I want to wait for Tracey."

"That would take a miracle, my friend."

"Exactly."

*****

Jeremy ran after the rotting cowboy until he could no longer keep up and then stopped, winded, hands on his knees. The cowboy kept trotting towards the horizon, without a backwards glance. Jeremy followed the hoof prints until darkness, then huddled into the grass to pass the cold night as best he could. He resisted the temptation to expect coyote calls, being another planet instead of a cowboy movie.

At dawn he resumed his track, the hoof prints still clearly visible. Two hours after sunrise, he heard the beat of hooves again, and the cowboy appeared holding the reins of another saddled horse.

"Thought we could get there faster if you were mounted, compadre," the cowboy drawled.

Jeremy gratefully but clumsily mounted, having never ridden a horse before. Within minutes of his horse following the other rider, his kidneys were jarred and his bottom battered. No amount of shifting in the saddle worked for long.

"What is your name?" he asked, trying to get his mind off his nethers.

"Bob," the man said with a sidelong glance. "You?"

"Jeremy Springs."

Bob cocked his head for a moment. "I knew someone named Springs once. Dem fine woman."

"How far off is your town?" Jeremy asked.

"A fur piece. Why, you in a hurry?"

"My ass is," Jeremy quipped.

Bob chortled. "Don't worry, me 'ansome, it'll get numb soon. Or we can canter instead of trot."

They rode on, a bit faster without the jarring trot. Jeremy tried to determine their direction of travel by looking at the sun angle, but remembered that on this planet it was not a given that the rotation was in the same direction as Earth. He also did not remember whether he was in the northern or southern hemisphere. They were on grassland, with gentle rolling hills. He squinted in their direction of travel, trying to see a town in the distance but could see nothing.

"Are we even going to your town?"

"Not dreckly. Need to meet up with the herd for the drive first. Once a year we send up a few thousand head to the weird beehive city. I hear they grind 'em up for the big sponge bitch. I doubt she lets the people there have anything good of it."

"Sponge bitch?"

Bob rotated his upper body in the saddle and regarded him.

"You really aren't from here, are you? There's a giant ocean that makes up most of this planet, and most of that is taken up by a sponge that runs things. I used to work for her, but that went out a' joint. She kidnapped the ancestors of these yokels and brought 'em here. You too, I imagine."

"You imagine right. But I'm going back."

The cowboy snorted. "Oh yeah? You happen to have a spaceship, me bey?"

"Not presently. But I plan on going to that beehive city or wherever and getting one."

The cowboy rode on in silence for a while, thinking. Jeremy let him ponder.

"How you plan on doing that?" he finally asked.

"I don't know, maybe I was hoping you would help me. Maybe we could all go back to Earth."

"Look, Jeremy Springs, we been here for near on a hundred and forty years. And in all that time nobody has tried to shanghai a spaceship. I used to pilot them, but I know enough to know I couldn't grab one alone, even if I wasn't in this condition. And not only that, but one would have to be on the ground somewhere to grab it. They aren't always. And who knows whether the soldiers would scat us all down in the meantime?"

"What's wrong with you all?" Jeremy scolded. "Are you Americans or what? What happened to 'We'll figure it out as we go along'? What happened to 'Give me liberty or give me death'? What happened to the good ol' American gumption?"

The cowboy rotated in his saddle to look back at Jeremy, scowling. After regarding him for a moment, he pulled his hat tighter and resumed riding, slumped over.

"I reckon you right, me 'ansome. Come with me."

The cowboy spurred his horse and broke into a gallop, veering left on a new course. Jeremy swallowed and kicked his horse too, hoping his horse would know to follow in spite of his ignorance of riding. Galloping proved easier riding than trotting or cantering, to his surprise. Before long he saw the dark outline of buildings on the horizon, and soon they were riding into a western town right out of central casting. There were clap-boarded stores, swing-doored saloons, livery stables, blacksmiths, mercantiles, and wooden houses. He did not see a church or a school, however. Cornish Bob rode to the sheriff's office and hitched his horse to a post. Jeremy incorrectly remembered horses stopped by pulling back on the reins, and did so, hard. The horse overreacted and reared, dumping Jeremy off over the withers and onto his backside. He rolled to the side to avoid being trampled.

Bob guffawed. "You'll get the hang of it. Welcome to New Bodie! Come on, we need to talk to Sheriff Dolan."

Jeremy stood, beating the dust off his paper coveralls, and they walked through the door of the sheriff's office. Sheriff Dolan was a stout man with a bushy, black mustache, and was wearing a round bowler hat and striped shirt with vest. He regarded Jeremy with a rheumy gaze.

"Morning, Cornish Bob. Who the hell is this?"

"This here is an American spaceman," Bob announced. "He's going to fly us all back to America."

"Is this true, boy?"

"Uh, yes sir," Jeremy bluffed, remembering that Bob had told him he could pilot it himself. "You just get me on a ship and we're as good as home."

"Well I'll be a son of a bitch," said Sheriff Dolan, slamming his hand on his desk. "Back to America, instead of being that bitch's bitches!"

"Exactly! Yes sir!" shouted Cornish Bob.

"So how are we gonna pull this off?" asked the Sheriff.

"I figure we drive the cattle up to the city like every year, but this time we go heeled. Instead of just dropping the cows off and coming back, this time we keep going, pull our pistols and storm the place. I know sometimes she has soldiers around, with better guns than ours, but if we take 'em by surprise we'll have a chance. Better than living like slaves here for the next generation, right?"

"Right you are, Bob. That's a hell of a plan. Let's go round up a posse and break out the Colts."

The Sheriff removed a key from his desk and opened a gun cabinet. They loaded a number of western-style pistols into a burlap sack.

"Best take a few repeaters too, Sheriff. Maybe we can have some lads give us cover from afar."

The Sheriff nodded and removed some Henry lever-action rifles as well.

"Don't forget the shells," Bob reminded.

Once they had two sacks filled with weaponry, the three of them walked to the town square, and the Sheriff pulled a rope connected to an iron bell. The urgent clanging soon had the whole town scrambling to join them in a mob.

"Where's the fire, Dolan?" one of them called.

"Ain't no fire. We need some men folk to volunteer for the Army. We're going to war against the sponge. This here boy is an American spaceman who knows how to fly them big transport ships. All we gotta do is shoot our way into the city and hogtie one."

"What if there ain't a big ship landed?" a woman asked.

"Well then we take a little one, load up some of the boys, and fly up and get a big one."

"What if there ain't a little one landed?"

The Sheriff placed his arms akimbo. "Well then, Mr. Tanner, we take some of them hive people hostage and trade for one. Look, it's about time we get the hell off this rock and get back to the U.S. of A."

"Hell yeah, I say," chimed in one of the townsfolk.

"Hell *no*, I say," argued a tall townsman with a round hat. "Why the hell would you want to leave here? We have it good, everything we need, with no gub'mint interference. Why ride off with the Sheriff and get yourselves kilt for nothing?"

Sheriff Dolan narrowed his eyes with a scowl. "You want to be slaves to that sponge forever, instead of getting back to California Territory? What the hell is wrong with you, Jimmy?"

"Nuthin' wrong with me, Sheriff Dolan. I just don't want to die with all you fools."

"You are a coward son of a bitch, Jimmy."

"No, you are a fool son of a bitch, you…" he cast about for a more potent expletive but failed and settled on volume, "…*son of a bitch!*"

"Well you just stay here cowering and be a bitch," said the Sheriff.

"I will," said Jimmy. "And I guess I'll have to be the sheriff after you hotheads get yourselves kilt."

"You just do that, Jimmy. After we get a ship, we'll come back and pick up any women and children who want to go back to America. We won't be picking up any cowardly men who didn't man up and ride with us though. Y'all can stay here with Yellow Jimmy and live the rest of your lives in servitude to a monster."

"I'll ride with you," said a townsman.

"I'm with you too," said another. Soon there was general hooting and hollering of support.

"All right then, men, gird yer' damn loins and mount up," shouted the Sheriff.

Half of the townsmen were willing, while the rest slunk off with Jimmy to the saloon. Before long, twenty-seven men kissed their wives and children and were mounted, armed, and riding out of town. They reached the cattle herd at sundown and armed the other herdsman. They passed the night around campfires, passing bottles of whiskey between them and keeping their spirits high with jovial bluster. In the morning, after shivering through the night in his papery coveralls, Jeremy rubbed his bloodshot eyes and pounding head while the townsfolk stirred the embers of the fires into life to make coffee and breakfast.

"You look cold, son," said Bob.

"Yeah. Wish I had thought to get some clothes in town," Jeremy answered.

"Probably would have been a good idea. But then you wouldn't be able to rally the troops as 'the spaceman.' But you don't have a belt for a pistol, though. Maybe you should carry one of the rifles; they have slings."

"Works for me," said Jeremy, hearkening back to his marksmanship training in the Marine Training Depot. Bob tossed him a Henry repeating rifle, and after breakfast he slung it over his shoulder, mounted his horse with aching buttocks, and joined the rest of the men as they drove the thundering herd of mooing cattle towards the rising sun.

The air warmed, bringing with it the ripe smell of bovine bodies and droppings. Towards mid-morning, Jeremy caught a glint of light in the sky, reflecting off of something. Worried about aircraft, he craned his neck to see what the source was. It soon became apparent that it was not a high-flying aircraft but a shiny dragonfly that was keeping pace with the herd. One of the cowboys caught sight of it.

"Oh shit, boys, a dragonfly drone! Hide yer' guns!"

"What's going on?" Jeremy asked Bob.

"The hive people use those to spy. They are little robots with cameras and such. Well, so much for the element of surprise if they see our pieces. Not much you can do about yours—you don't even have pockets."

Jeremy's stomach fell when he saw the little drone dip and hover towards him. It hovered over his head.

"Holy crap," he whispered. "Should I shoot it?"

"Naw. Too late now," said Bob. "Maybe just bluff it out; they may think we have guns for coyotes. Even though there ain't no coyotes on this planet."

A tiny speaker crackled to life on the drone, and a tinny little voice spoke.

"Jeremy Springs, as I live and breathe. It took long enough to track you down, you lazy asshole."

Jeremy's mind reeled, trying to place the voice. "Chris? Is that you?"

*****

Chris huddled over the screen and clumsily manipulated the drone's controls while Elanor tried to grab them from her hands.

"Stop it!" she protested.

"Stop what?" replied Jeremy's voice from the speaker. "Should we abort the mission?"

"Not you, Jeremy. My friend Elanor who thinks she can handle this drone better than I can."

"So we are still a 'go,' then. Good. So what do we do now?"

"What were *you* planning?" Chris asked.

"We were going to ride to the city like they always do driving the cattle but this time shoot the place up and grab a transport ship."

Chris shook her head in disbelief. "That was it? That was your big plan?"

Jeremy shrugged. "You have a better idea?"

"Well I do now. How about we give you some over-watch and let you know where and who to attack? And maybe try to make sure there is a ship on the ground?"

"That would be most helpful."

"You're welcome. Just keep riding and we'll get back to you with a target."

"Roger," said Jeremy with a salute.

They ordered the drone to return to its hanger outside the City of God.

"Wow, this is exciting," said Elanor, clapping her hands.

"So now," said Chris, "we have to figure out a way to make sure a transport ship is on the ground near the city and maybe that it isn't guarded, round up all the members of the Virii, and figure out how to fly the transport up here to get us off the orbiting station. We have to destroy the station and figure out how to fly us all back to Earth. Am I missing anything?"

Elanor shoved her chair against Chris's and moved her from the screen. She cracked her knuckles then began tapping at the keyboard.

"There. In two days' time, the transport ship Glow of Power will land just outside the City of God to pick up Rosa 40, Cain 10, Valentina 69, and Anton 36 for penal transport to the giant scorpion beach. The members of our cell have all been ordered to report there, so they will all be on board when your brother and his band of cowherders attacks and brings the ship up here to get us. We alter the course of the orbiting manufacturing facility to crash it into the sea."

"I had no idea you were such a hacker."

"I'm not. There are no protections on the computers. All the people using them are drugged up and worship Eiffeila as a Goddess, so there is no need for any codes. Heck, most of her people are too drugged up to remember things anyway."

"So at that point we will be floating in a stolen ship with a whole fleet of pissed-off sponge warriors ready to blast us to dust. What then?"

"We fly to Earth of course."

"How?"

"Anton 36 is a shuttle pilot, remember? He'll fly us."

Chris blinked. "This is all so...easy. Too easy."

Elanor flexed her eyebrows. "Nothing is hard when you are not drugged on Xylol."

Chris finished her shift and returned to her bunk. The next day's shift passed with glacial slowness. She could not sleep the night before the hijacking and passed the time watching reruns of "Super Powerful Anti-Demon Special Warrior Force Attack!" on the television.

The morning came without fanfare. Chris walked to the workstation and found Elanor already piloting the dragonfly drone. She crowded into the space in front of the screen and saw that the dragonfly drone was hovering over a mid-sized transport ship. Elanor pivoted the camera and showed the herd of cattle with the cowboy escort just cresting a rolling hill in the distance, approaching the ship and the town.

"Good of you to wake up and join us," Elanor said archly.

"I wasn't sleeping. And thanks for waiting for me. Are we on board the ship yet?"

"Everyone but Valentina. But she's still missing, so no surprise there. Your brother is going to be clever about this, I trust?"

"I hope so. What have you told him?"

"Nothing yet. Let's fly over and plan."

Elanor manipulated the keyboard, and the dragonfly drone shot across the plain towards the cattle herd. Jeremy was riding a horse at the head of the cavalcade, with a few other cowboys. She squinted when she noticed one of them was a rotting skeleton. The rest were driving the herd from the rear and containing the sides.

"Good morning, my idiot brother," Chris spoke into the screen.

"And a fair fine morning to you, my snide sister," she heard Jeremy retort. "So is that the ship you have so cleverly provided for us ahead there?"

"Yes," Chris answered. "It has...how many crew?" she asked, turning to Elanor."

"Three," she answered.

"It has three crewmen on board," Chris repeated to Jeremy. "I'm thinking you drive the cows right past the front of the ship. Just climb on board and take out the crew, throw them out the door into the herd, and then get the rest of your cowboys on board too. Anton will fly you up here. With any luck you can do the whole thing without firing a shot."

"You make it sound so easy. What are they armed with?" Jeremy asked.

Elanor shrugged. "Guns?"

"Guns," Chris answered.

"Thank you. Very helpful. Very specific," Jeremy said with a salute.

Chris scowled. "Just do your Marine thing, a-hole."

Elanor piloted the dragonfly drone back towards the ship to give them a better vantage point. The transport ship was parked just off the road, a mile from the outer fringes of the City of God. They watched as the herd approached, now with six cowboys and the zombie in front with Jeremy.

"Can you get closer so we can see and hear?" Chris asked Elanor.

"Sure."

The dragonfly drone floated just behind the cowboys as they led the herd past the open doors of the transport ship then dismounted and entered it. The screen jostled for a moment then showed Jeremy approaching two of the crewmen inside the ship. They too wore papery coveralls but were soldiers by their muscular statures and face paint.

"Good morning," said Jeremy, as the other cowboys spread out into the vestibule. "Where should we take these cows?"

The two soldiers glanced at each other, confused.

"Now boys, git 'em!" yelled one of the cowboys, and the fight was on. The camera on the dragonfly drone was jostled, so they missed most of the brawl, but it stabilized in time to see the two soldiers dragged unconscious out the door into the herd. Cain 10 appeared, dragging what Chris presumed to be the pilot, and threw his inert form out to join the soldiers. Cain appeared to have been struck in the face, perhaps by one of the cowboys who assumed he was one of the soldiers. The drone showed the rest of the cowboys crowding into the ship and Rosa 40 escorting them into the cargo bay. The drone followed over Jeremy's shoulder as he made his way with Cain 10 to the bridge, where Anton 36 sat in the pilot's chair.

"Are we all on board?" Anton asked.

"Ready to fly," answered Cain.

Anton manipulated a slider, and the main screen powered on. It showed a large, curved surface at the bottom of the screen, which Chris assumed was a representation of the planet's surface. Several lights circled above, probably satellites and other ships.

"Let's get out of here before they notice us," growled Anton. He started manipulating various controls.

"Where we headin'?" asked one of the cowboys.

"Up to the orbiting Xylol manufacturing facility to pick up the rest of my group," answered Anton.

"No sir. Not until you fly out to my town and we pick up the rest of our families," stated the cowboy.

"We don't have time for this," Anton argued.

"Well, then, make time for it," Jeremy ordered. "Sheriff Dolan is right. This was part of the deal."

"Not my deal," said Anton.

"It is now, son," drawled the Sheriff, resting his hand on his revolver.

"Now everyone calm down," Chris said through the drone speaker. "We have time to go get your people, Sheriff Cowboy. I trust your families will be ready to go immediately. Go on Anton, fly over there."

"Where is this town?" Anton asked.

"Head east, about two days' ride."

Anton smirked. "How far is 'two days' ride' in non-primitive-savage terms?"

"Just fly east, Tussbucket," Cornish Bob growled.

Anton lifted the transport off, and they banked to their left. Within ten minutes they had spotted the town on the screen ahead.

Suddenly alarm klaxons blared.

"Dammit, did they find us out?" Cain said.

"I don't think so," Anton answered, puzzled. "That's a military alert."

Anton adjusted the screen. The scale had broadened to show the planet as a much smaller circle near the center of the screen. Hundreds of lights flashed like stars at all points.

"Are those...?" asked Jeremy.

"Yeah. Enemy ships. We are under a massive Demon attack."

*****

Smithson wrapped the lone remaining LaGrue's damaged robotic arm around his shoulder and helped him hobble towards a massive door. He helped himself to two of the pistols and some magazines from the multitude of dead LaGrues that littered the floor.

"Where are you hurt?" he asked.

LaGrue checked himself. "Looks like none of the damage was life critical. Artificial lungs intact, circulation operational. Just power supply backup and locomotion damage. Some reduction in strength amplification."

"Good. Where can we go to talk without being interrupted by any more of you?" Smithson asked.

"I know a place—but no, my others would think of that. You better choose."

Smithson led them randomly down several massive stone halls filled with LaGrue busts and portraits of him in heroic battle scenes. They came to a door in an alcove and entered. It appeared to be the quarters of a worker, which was unoccupied.

"This will do for now," said Smithson, and eased LaGrue into a wooden chair by a rough table. LaGrue heaved a ragged breath.

"What am I going to do?"

"Interesting you said 'I' instead of 'we,'" Smithson said.

"It is odd," said LaGrue with a wry smile. "I am a series of individuals, not connected like Eiffelia is. That is how she is able to match me. She can stay connected across times and universes in a way that I cannot. But she cannot best me because each of my selves is independently operational without the others. Any one of us can duplicate into hundreds of other LaGrues, each with a rift generator of his own. We should be unstoppable! But...."

Smithson held his tongue, allowing LaGrue to finish the thought.

"But so can she, using her minions! Every time we engage, we quickly reach infinite regress, each trying to out-produce the other with rift generators, with fleets of starships, going back farther and farther in time to cut off her slaves from being born, her planets from populating, her stars even from forming! And always competing for full Pangborn carriers. It is madness! And when I don't engage her? Even worse madness. Building all these monuments to myself, building empires to worship me with my godlike power? It's...horrible. I have to stop it. *We* have to stop it."

"How will you convince all of the LaGrues to help you?"

"We are all the same. If I have come to this conclusion given this set of facts, they will all come to the same one too."

"But will they all believe you?"

"Of course. I have seen what I have seen, and each of them can independently observe the same thing for themselves. What I had been missing was a certain point of view to observe the facts from."

"I think," said Smithson, sitting at the table across from LaGrue, "that you are going to have a harder time convincing all the rest of the LaGrues to end things than you think."

"What do you mean?"

Smithson pursed his lips and exhaled.

"Look, I am not one of the Mods who know things. I'm just a low-level operative, but I know what I know. And I know that once you split your ego into others, the clone aspect only goes so far. From the moment you duplicate, you have a complete, self-sufficient, new human there who has its own perspective and experiences that are not shared. Even with identical brains, the patterns that develop are only so similar. And the egos are entirely dissimilar."

"We are similar enough that we think the same way and the same things. We are fundamentally the same person, split into many."

Smithson stroked his beard briskly. "Think of it this way. You are going to be asking another you to end this game. What if one of your other yous asked you to do it? Would you?"

"Of course! As long as there is one of us to continue on."

Smithson squinted. "Wait, are we talking about the same thing?"

"We are going to commit mass suicide," blinked LaGrue. "Only one of us should continue. It is the natural order."

"Whoa there, compadre. Why don't you just destroy all the rift generators but one and have all you LaGrues live out your natural—I mean, un-natural lives—here on LaGrue world? What would that hurt? The game would end without the lemming part."

"That's a myth, by the way," LaGrue instructed. "Lemmings don't commit mass suicide."

"Then why should you?

LaGrue slumped, pondering. "Even though we are duplicates of the same ego, we are different. I would have a hard time turning myself over to non-existence, even though without one of my predecessor LaGrues I would not exist. I'm not sure any of us even know at this point who the original one is. We all just sort of wake up after a jump back to duplicate, each with a slightly different set of memories. I remember setting out to duplicate and having three of me materialize. We then all jumped and picked up a fifth. So with an incredible amount of reconstructing memories, assuming every one of us was completely honest, we could in theory reconstruct which one of us was the original LaGrue. Assuming he is not one of us locked into an infinite regress line with Eiffelia. There must be an easier way."

"You are assuming," said Smithson, "that the LaGrue who ultimately gets to live your old life and return the rift generator to Ron must be the original one. Why is that?"

"It seems a fair way to determine who lives out of this."

"You are all the same. You might as well choose by chance."

"As distasteful as that sounds, I see no logical reason not to," nodded LaGrue. "What we need is a way to ensure that none of me is tempted to cheat and live on with a rift generator. What would be the best outcome is one that also annihilates Eiffelia in the bargain."

"I'm pretty sure that won't happen, no matter how you play this. She has been playing this game for a long, long time."

LaGrue stroked his chin. "You are correct, of course. But perhaps I can hurt her, set her back. Perhaps if I plunged a ship with a rift generator onboard into the sun of each known system where she has a planet with an ocean that she uses as a home location? The resultant supernovae would wipe out the whole system, her sponge body with it."

Smithson raised his eyebrows. "That sounds pretty drastic. What about the other inhabitants of the planets in those systems?"

"Her modus operandi is to operate without any intelligent life in the vicinity of her sponge bodies, with the exception of some captive populations of slaves drugged beyond salvage to make sure she is fed and defended. I am willing to sacrifice them in order to achieve my objective. Even if she survives in some locations that are unknown to me, the eradication of most of her entire systems and the slaves she has cultivated will set her back for generations."

Smithson scowled. "Well perhaps I am *not* willing to allow you to sacrifice them. They might be drugged thralls, but they are sentient beings capable of healing from her drugs."

LaGrue steepled his hands and nodded. "I appreciate your position and will consider the possibility of another solution."

Smithson narrowed his eyes, untrusting. It occurred to him that LaGrue might well carry out this plan, but the only way to stop him would be to immediately kill him. But it further occurred to him that should he do this, the other LaGrues and their minions would likely capture him and the entire scene would repeat. The situation had a momentum beyond his control.

"What are you going to do with me?" Smithson asked.

"I will take you to wherever you ask and leave you."

Smithson considered. He needed to report this situation to the Mods. "I would like you to take me to a Chinese restaurant in Seattle called House of Kong."

"An odd request, but done."

*****

Valentina Pavlov shaded her eyes and tried to continue reading the children's book, but the setting sun and her tears were making it difficult. She looked out across the vast city from the vast stone patio attached to the vast LaGrue bedroom with the massive LaGrue statues and let out a shuddering breath.

"Mommy?"

"Yes, Mandy?"

"I don't like it here either. The only thing I like about it is I don't have to be Mandy 42 anymore, just Mandy."

"Yes. That is the nice part."

"But LaGrue is just as bad a boss as Eiffelia, isn't he?"

"Yes honey. Just different."

"Yeah. We don't have to pretend we are stupid and drugged any more, but we have to pretend we like LaGrue like everyone else does. It is the same."

LaGrue popped into existence before them, making them jump.

"I hate it when he does that, Mommy."

"Me too, sweetie."

"Good evening, wife," he said.

"I am not your wife," Valentina mumbled.

"Of course you are," LaGrue countered. "Even though you are not happy about it. But you will be happy to know that our relationship will soon change."

She waited, trying to gauge his mood and meaning from his bearing. He seemed pensive and a bit wistful.

"We will soon end our war with Eiffelia by sacrificing all of me but one. We have all decided. By the operation of random choice, I have been selected as the only surviving LaGrue. The rest of me are even now as we speak piloting vast armadas of our ships to attack every known homeworld of Eiffelia. We will pilot our ships into their suns and destroy her utterly. Only I will be left. We will take a ship and use the rift generator to insert into the world line where we were working at the base under the Denver Airport—the last time we were together without two or more of me. The only change will be that we will replace our versions of ourselves at that point, which will likely be enough to start a new world line in which we will be married. Mandy will be our child. We will decline to join Ron and Tracey when Cornish Bob attacks them and will thus not participate in that world line. We will live happily for the rest of our lives."

Valentina sat quietly, digesting this.

"I do not understand what you mean by 'replace' our versions in that world line. Do you mean they will just pop out of existence when we get there?"

"Of course not. We will have to replace them by posing as ourselves. Those old versions must be removed."

"What do you mean 'removed'? That is no better than saying 'replaced.' Just say it: Do you mean they will be killed?"

"Of course," LaGrue spat. "But that is ok, we are the same people, just from farther in the future."

"You are a monster."

Why are you so difficult? You have no choice here. You will obey me. Once we are inserted into the new timeline, if you tell anyone about this, they will think you insane."

"And what makes you think I won't just divorce you at that point?"

LaGrue seemed genuinely surprised. "Why would you do that? Have I not treated you like the queen you are? What is so bad about me? I do not understand you."

"And you never have, fool."

LaGrue started to storm off but caught himself.

"Well we shall see how this turns out. We are leaving."

"When?"

"Now. This instant. Gather what things you need."

"I have nothing to gather," Valentina whispered.

"Then come with me to the end of the patio," he said, grabbing her arm.

Valentina took Mandy's hand in her free arm, and they walked to the edge of the stone patio. LaGrue spoke into his rift generator. A short time later, a large ship flew into view and came to hover at the end of the patio. A walkway was extended from a door that opened in the ship, and another LaGrue emerged and joined them.

"Greetings, Most Fortunate!" he said, a bit over-enthusiastically. "I bring you your chariot to begin your new lives."

The surviving LaGrue beamed with pleasure. "Thank you, Sacrificer. Have you made the modifications which will return the rift generator to you after delivering us to our timeline?"

"Indeed, Fortunate, I have programmed the ship to drop you off, wait five minutes for you to exit, then return here."

"Excellent work, Sacrificer. May your end be glorious!"

"And may your life be long and grand, Fortunate One!"

The survivor LaGrue escorted Valentina and Mandy down the gangplank. Out of the corner of her eye Valentina caught an odd expression on the other LaGrue's face.

Is he hiding something?

The ship itself seemed oddly familiar in outline. She wondered why.

"Have a seat while I seal the hull, wife."

"Wait...."

LaGrue ignored her, and busied about the control room. Then it occurred to her where she had seen the ship.

"Wait!"

The ship made the jump at that moment. They were thrown into the nauseating effects and were left writhing on the floor.

"Can...can a rift generator be made to self-destruct?" she panted.

"I suppose it can," he answered, groaning.

"Will it explode or make a rift?"

"I don't know. Why?"

"He wasn't sending us back to when we were investigating the wrecked ship and the rift under the airport. He sent us back to *be* the ship and make the rift. He's going to kill you. And us. No survivors, no new timeline. He's rigged the ship to blow a rift open and throw the hulk into that new universe. They decided without you to all go down."

"That's....but why?"

She could only shake her head before the explosion took them.

—10—

"This control room is too crowded—I need most of you to clear out. At least the corpse. He stinks," Anton complained.

Anton had landed the transport ship near the town, and the Sheriff left to round up the townsfolk.

"What is going on up there?" Chris fidgeted, looking over Anton's shoulder at the display screen.

Anton pointed to the screen with the hundreds of points of light slowly circling the planet and the sun at its center.

"I'm not sure at this point. They aren't attacking anything, but Eiffelia hasn't put up any ships to fight them. I think if we can get the hell out of here we might be able to slip through before any shooting starts."

"We still need to crash the Xylol 23 factory," Elanor demanded.

"I think those demon ships will handle that for us," Jeremy said. "We just need to get the hell out of here."

"Ang on there me 'ansums, there is something afoot that 'ol Bob can smell even beyond his own corruption. Tune your communications to a broad band to see if we can pick up some discourse between the Demons and the sponge."

Anton touched the screen, and shortly voices were heard.

"...then we are at an impasse," said the unmistakable voice of Eiffelia.

"Not at all," answered a voice vaguely familiar only to Cornish Bob. "There is only one outcome to this. One of my ships will make it through whatever you throw at us and will plunge into your sun. The resultant meltdown of the ship's rift generator will trigger a supernova which will cause each rift generator in all of my ships to supernovae by chain reaction. The resultant cluster of supernovae will incinerate this entire planetary system and all nearby."

"You are willing to end our war in this way, Professor LaGrue?" asked Eiffelia.

Cornish Bob slapped his forehead, dislodging gobs of flesh. *That's who it is!*

"I am. And as you no doubt can detect, this scene is being enacted on as many of your host planets in as many world lines as I have been able to discover in the course of our eternal war. I am not foolish enough to assume that I have discovered all of your planetary systems, but I might have. And at the very least this will hurt you. Badly."

Eiffelia laughed. "You are indeed a fool. Of course you do not know all of my home worlds throughout all timelines and universes. All I will have to do is start rebuilding on the surviving timelines retroactively then expand again into whatever you have destroyed. Your gesture here is empty. We will be back to our exquisitely enjoyable infinite regressive conflicts in no time at all."

"Of course I will not destroy you. That is a hope but not an expectation here. I am doing this to destroy *me*."

There was silence on the airway for long seconds.

"You are...quitting?" Eiffelia asked. "How selfish of you. Not only will you deprive me a great deal of pleasure by ending our game, but have you thought about all the poor human slaves on my home worlds that service me? Millions will die."

"Unfortunate collateral damage," LaGrue deadpanned. "They were casualties the minute you took and bred them. As was I."

"You're bluffing," Eiffelia stammered.

A burst of static indicated that LaGrue had severed the communication.

"He's not bluffing," Bob announced with a shake of his head. "We need to get out of here."

"Not without the townsfolk," said Jeremy.

"Fuck the savages! We need to take off right now!" Anton growled, reaching for the controls.

"Not so hasty," drawled Cornish Bob, drawing his revolver and pressing it against Anton's head. "Jeremy, me bey, please go urge the Sheriff to convince the good residents of New Bodie to get on the ship immediately or be blown into their component atoms."

Jeremy's eyes widened and he slipped from the control room.

"We need to leave them. We don't have time!" Anton protested.

"We have a little," argued Cornish Bob. "I know Professor LaGrue a wee bit, and even though he is a cold and calculating eel, even he will take a few minutes to proverbially screw his courage to the sticking point. As long as Eiffelia doesn't press the matter by taking a pot shot at 'im."

"Are you willing to bet your life on that?" said Anton, in a near panic.

"Are you?" countered Bob, cocking the hammer of his pistol.

Jeremy chose that moment to stick his head back into the control room.

"We got 'em. All that would come, anyway. We're not going to convince Tanner and some of his boys. They were up at the saloon and wouldn't budge."

"Their loss then," said Bob, holstering his Colt. "Let's go."

Anton raised the gangplank door and lifted the ship off.

"Wait, I've thought of something else," Cornish Bob announced.

"The hell you say," said Anton, continuing the flight.

"Yes, the hell I say," said Bob, unholstering his pistol again. "I need to get a piece of Eiffelia. A hunk of wall from the City of God will do. We have to have some leverage when that mad professor blows her up."

"Are you insane?" shouted Anton.

"Maybe! We'll see. I think you will have reason to thank me. Take us close to a wall and hover where I can reach it from the gangplank. Or I will put a round in your brainpan and pilot the ship there meself. Don't argue and dawdle, time's a' wastin."

Anton calculated his odds of survival rapidly, then veered the ship towards Eiffelia's city. He brought the ship to a level hover near a rounded tower and extended the gangplank.

"Go ahead, get your chunk," he spat.

Cornish Bob chuckled. "You mean *we* will go get our chunk. I don't think I'll give you the chance of just blasting away while I'm at the end of the gangplank, me bey."

Cornish Bob marched Anton through the ship and down the gangplank to where it hovered next to a white, curved wall of the City of God. He shot the wall into some recoverable fragments.

"Grab 'em and let's fly," he ordered.

Anton complied, leaning out while Bob held on to his belt. They returned to the control room, Bob pocketing the fragments.

Elanor pointed to the display screen. "One of the ships is breaking free and starting towards the sun."

"That's it!" hollered Bob. "He's starting his move. We need to jump somewhere. Anywhere. *Now.*"

Anton made rapid adjustments on the screen, and all but Bob abruptly felt the effects of a rift jump. Bob shouldered Anton from the control chair while he still reeled with nausea, then manipulated the screen view.

"Where are we?" he mumbled.

"Ten light years out," groaned Anton.

"That'll do for now," said Bob cheerily. "Now we decide where to take everyone."

"Back to the U.S. of A.," croaked the Sheriff, recovering. "Where our ancestors were shanghaied, Bodie California Territory. What year to you suggest?"

"Let's put you at the start of things, in 1875," Bob said, rubbing his chin. "May I suggest prospecting up on the bluff?"

"For Jeremy and me," Chris said, "AUTEC, Andros Island in the Caribbean, year 2017."

"Very well," said Bob. "And what of your merry band of former Eiffelia lackeys?" he asked Elanor.

"I have no idea," she said, shaking her head. "Why don't you leave us with the ship when you get off and we can talk about it later."

Bob raised what was left of his eyebrows. "Why me pretty poppet, whatever makes you think I am getting off of this ship?"

"This is our ship," Anton growled. "*We* stole it."

"That you did," Bob agreed. "But now I am stealing it." He abruptly pulled his pistol and shot Anton in the forehead.

The shot echoed in the control room, and they reacted with shock as Anton collapsed from the chair, blood geysering from his head.

The Sheriff growled and grabbed at the butt of his pistol.

"Ah ah ah, Sheriff, tut tut!" Cornish Bob laughed. "Please keep in mind that I am the only pilot on this ship floating in the middle of time and space, and unless you all want to remain that way until someone figures out how to fly this thing...and I assure you that if you manage to do that it will be a long, long time and the results of your attempts could be catastrophic."

Sheriff Dolan eased his hand off his pistol, muttering.

"A wise choice, me beauty. Now for the rest of you, I will just have to take you somewhere and allow me to save the day against the evil sponge by keeping the ship. Do you have a preference, or should you just get off with one of the other groups?"

Elanor looked between Rosa and Cain.

"I'm up for cowboy land," she said. "I'll play my cards there."

"I'm game," said Rosa. "Maybe knowing what I do about medicine I could help the sick."

"Sounds good," nodded Cain. "Maybe I can make something of myself by having an advantage with that level of technology."

"Then it's settled." Bob smacked his lips with zealous satisfaction. He started manipulating the screen. "You kids just head down the hall to the hold and join the other cowpokes, and I'll land you just outside of town."

The ship jumped again, and Bob piloted the ship from orbit down to the Pacific Ocean, then flew low across the California coast eastwards towards the Sierra Mountains. He flew across the high desert sage, past the tufa of Mono Lake, then up a slope on the south side of the lake. He hovered near the peak, hiding from the town on the north side.

"Out you go!" he said cheerily, extending the gangplank. They watched on the screen as the cowboys and the Virii disembarked.

"I'm sure they will all end up being the movers and shakers of Bodie," Bob d knowingly. "It's just us three," he said to Chris and Jeremy, closing the hatch. "Now where did you say you wanted to go?"

Jeremy and Chris took their turn exchanging glances. "We thought you could drop up back where we were taken from. It's an island in the Caribbean called Andros and has some kind of secret government base on it."

Bob froze, his glassy eyes becoming even more filmy. He pivoted around in his chair and regarded Chris and Jeremy carefully.

"Where have I heard that island's name before?" he mused. He tilted his head. Seconds passed. He abruptly straightened.

"Of course. It's been a few years, but it all makes sense. What did you say your last names are?"

"Springs," they said in unison.

"And your mother's name wouldn't happen to be *Tracey* Springs, would it?"

"Uh—yes. How did you know that?" Chris answered.

"Well me poppets, it just so happens that I am an ol' pal of your mother. I believe that instead of taking you to your sunny island, I shall take you directly to her. After."

"After what?"

"Why, after making myself presentable, of course. I am a stink'n corpse at the moment, as you no doubt have noticed."

"Yeah, we noticed all right," complained Chris. "How exactly are you going to remedy that?"

"Well, let me just fill you in a bit on ol' Cornish Bob's history. Without waxin' too full, I came from Bodie here not too far off in the future from where we sit now. In fact, I anticipate your friends meeting me at some point in their future and my past there in town. Anyhoo, I ended up going through a rift and getting mixed up with the evil sponge. I was one of her goons for many years, and part of the deal I was turned into a living dead body. That allowed me to go on gooning for many more years than we usually get, as long as we get to soak to keep our cells in a state of arrested decay! After a while, circumstances involving your dear Ma and her chunder-tuss boyfriend who happens also to be my great-great-grand-boy, freed me from her bondage. At that time, I returned to Bodie at some time in our current near future and tried to hide out from Eiffelia and her new goons. As part of my hideout plans, I included a vat of the chemical solution that kept me from decaying. As you can see, my plan went awry, she found me, and returned me to the home planet you recently vacated. And as part of my punishment, the bitch removed my access to the rejuvenation vats. But now! Circumstances have again put a rift generator and ship into my soon-to-be formerly rotting hands!"

"So you are going to jump into the future from here and get into your vat," Jeremy deduced.

"Exactly! And once I am presentable, with the vat installed in the hold of this ship, we will then return you to your lovely family."

"And you will try to hide from her again? What makes you think it will work this time?"

"I don't. This time I will attempt to recruit your mother and my long lost grand-boy to help me get my revenge on the evil one."

—11—

The monkey man approached them. "Excuse me, Master Morrow and Mistress Springs, but there is a visitor at the door."

"Who is it?" asked Morrow.

"Mr. Smithson," answered the monkey man.

"Ah. Please show him in."

The monkey man exited with a barely perceptible bow and returned a short time later with Smithson.

"How are you, my friend?" greeted Morrow warmly.

"I am well, Andrew, and good to see you too, Tracey."

"And you too, Smithson," she said.

"I would love to catch up on the progress of your training, but there is an imminent danger that we must address," Smithson said. "The great war between Eiffelia and the LaGrues appears to be coming to a close."

"That sounds like a good thing!" answered Morrow.

"Yes, but the way LaGrue is planning to bring this about involves him diving rift generator-powered ships into the suns of as many of Eiffeila's systems as he can find. And he has found a great deal of them, over the millennia."

"Oh dear," said Morrow. "That will cause the suns to supernovae, killing not just her but whoever else is in that system, and possibly other systems nearby. Let me think on this."

Morrow paced the room slowly, chin in hand. "On the one hand, the damage he could do to Eiffelia would be significant, if not total. On the other, it might be completely futile should he not destroy all of her worlds. She would simply go back in time and build them back up. And, of course, the loss of innocent lives would also be catastrophic. We simply have to stop him."

"Agreed," said Smithson. "Do you have any ideas?"

"We will have to get to one of the LaGrues and convince him to stop," said Morrow.

"Easier said than done," observed Smithson. "Do you have a ship?"

"No. But Tracey was just about to dream one up."

Smithson raised his eyebrows and regarded Tracey

"Uh....what?" she said.

They laughed. "Is she done then? Fully trained now?" asked Smithson.

"Almost. Just have the fairy tale to tell." Morrow smiled.

"Ah yes. The story of life," said Smithson. "I remember this one."

"Wait a minute, said Tracey. "Do we have time for this? Don't we have a thousand supernovae fireballs to stop?"

"We have time," said Morrow. Time passes differently in Otherwhen locations like this. We can spend the next hundred years in here, and no time at all will have passed outside. Relax."

"Ok—so what is this story?"

"It is the end of training. Some truths can only be told through parable, tales, analogy. They can only be pointed at, not described."

"So will I be able to dream up a miracle ship after hearing this?" she said.

"Oh yes! Of course. And more!" chuckled Smithson.

"All right. I don't get this, as usual, and of course. But go ahead."

"The name of this tale is 'Jane and the Big Ball.'"

"This isn't a dirty story, is it?" Tracey asked.

Smithson scowled then chuckled.

"Once upon a time," began Morrow, "there was a poor young girl named Jane who lived in a cottage in the woods. Beyond the woods was the great castle in which lived the King and his Queen and their son the Prince, but Jane had never been to the castle and did not have many friends, for the forest was scantily populated. But she was friends with many of the forest animals and spirits. Every night of the year, the King would oversee his Grand Ball. All of his grand courtiers and nobles attended, but in addition, once every year, ten lucky commoners would be invited as well. The commoners would have a dreadful choice to make, however. The Ball would be wonderful and magical, full of experiences, romances, and delights! But at the end of the ball the next morning they would lose their lives!"

"That sucks," said Tracey.

"Hush," said Smithson. "No more balls jokes."

"One day, Jane was surprised by a knock at the door of her little cabin. She opened it and found a beautiful old woman with twinkling eyes and long, gray hair, dressed in the livery of a royal messenger. She was bearing an invitation to the grand ball! 'Oh dear,' said Jane, 'what should I do?'

"The royal messenger said, 'Fear not, for if you choose to join the Ball, you can join it at any time, and the Ball is, as you know, televised. You can watch the Ball in progress in order to help make your decision.'

"'I will do just that, it is one of my favorite shows,' she said.

"The royal messenger handed Jane the golden invitation. 'Be sure to watch the next episode! Of course, it is one thing to experience the Ball from afar, but actually being there is like nothing else!'

"The royal messenger mounted her steed and thundered away. Jane decided then and there, after watching the Ball from afar since she was a little girl, that she had no need to watch another episode. She decided she would indeed experience it for herself that very night!

"So Jane packed an apple, some cheese, and some bread in a kerchief and tied it to a stick, and locked her cottage behind her.

"As she walked through the woods on the way to the palace, she ran across her friend Bear digging into a rotting log for some grubs."

"'Where are you off to, Jane?' Bear asked.

"'I have a golden invitation to the Ball and am off to experience it.'

"'You are so fortunate! If I had an invitation, I would go straight for the refreshment tables. When I watch the show, I see the guests sipping fine champagne and eating tender morsels.'

"'Surely there is more to the Ball than that,' Jane said. 'Besides, sometimes the food and drink are in short supply. On one episode they ran out, and the guests were famished and picking at the crumbs!'

"'Yes, but even their hunger and thirst was delicious.'

"After walking a while further, Jane came across her friend Mouse.

"'Where are you bound, sister Jane?'

"'I am off to the Ball, for I have an invitation!'

"'You are so lucky! If I had a golden ticket, I would find friends and dance the night away!'

"'You would have to be careful, sister Mouse. I saw one episode where a small creature was stepped on during the dancing!'

"'Yes, but even being broken and watching from the wallboards would be sublime.'

"Jane grew hungry and stopped to untie her bundle. She nibbled on a corner of her cheese and was soon joined by her friend Crow.

"'Where are you off to, with your travel bag?' Crow asked.

"'I am off to the Ball, for I have a golden invitation!'

"'Oh I would just die for one!' cried the Crow. 'The library at the castle is grand and has many tomes, and I would read and read as long as I could!'

"'Yes, the library is wonderful, but I am afraid that I won't have time for much reading.'

"'Of course,' nodded Crow. 'But every minute spent in experiencing, sharing company, and learning would be bliss.'

"Jane continued her journey and neared the edge of the forest. Beyond lay farmlands, and in the distance she could just make out the pinnacles, towers, and battlements of the King's castle.

"The path she was following was joined by another path, and walking upon it was Jane's friend Jack. He too had a bundle tied to a stick on his shoulder and walked with purpose.

"'Good morning, Jack, where are you bound?' asked Jane.

"'I am on my way to the Ball, for I have a golden invitation,' he said.

"'That is wonderful, so am I!' said Jane. 'Perhaps we can go together?'

"'Sure,' said Jack. 'I was hoping someone I knew would be there. Maybe we can dance together, if I find the time.'

"'What do you mean?' asked Jane.

"'My friends all have urgings on what I should do there. Fox wants me to try to pitch a business deal to one of the rich nobles. Pike wants me to petition to the king about justice because of a legal dispute she is having with Hawk. And Moose wants me to say prayers at the chapel.'

"'My friends also have ideas on how I should attend the Ball,' Jane said. 'And they will be watching, along with millions of others.'

"They walked slowly through the stone-cobbled streets of the city towards the castle. They approached the bridge over the moat. They crossed the bridge and stood before the great oaken doors of the castle. The doors slowly and silently swung wide, revealing the doorman and the Ball in full swing within. The doorman reached out his hand.

"'Yes,' said Jack. 'But we are the ones with the golden invitations.'

"And they went inside."

Tracey sat in silence.

"That's it? That is the end of the story?"

"Yup," said Smithson. "Or the beginning rather."

"What happened next?" asked Tracey.

"They danced, of course," said Morrow.

Tracey pursed her lips. "Well I'm sure that is deep and all, but I don't get it. That was the most pointless ending to a story I have ever heard."

"You'll get it eventually. We are all either currying favor or favoring curry," said Smithson.

Tracey squinted her confusion. "So that's it? They dance and in the morning she dies?"

"Who said anything about her dying?" asked Smithson.

"You said she loses her life!" Tracey protested.

"You can lose your life and not die," Morrow said quietly. "She just didn't go back to her old life in her little cottage."

Tracey snapped her mouth shut. "Ok. It appears that I need an explanation of this parable. Jesus did that for his disciples, didn't he?"

"Oh fine," said Morrow, rolling his eyes. "The woods are the real world, where we are before coming into this world to live our lives. The real world is ruled over by the king God, his son the prince that he sent into our world to show the way and dance with us for a while, and the queen who ties them together with the kingdom. The Ball is this universe, our current reality, in which we come to experience, learn, and interact through and for love."

Tracey mulled this over, slightly dizzy and overwhelmed.

"And the animals? They watch us on tv?"

"Oh boy, do they ever watch!" said Smithson.

"How creepy. Don't they have their own lives there in the eternal forest beyond time and space?"

"Of a sort," said Morrow. "They do have time and space, but it is fuzzy and indefinite. What they lack, and why they tune in to the Ball, is the power of story, their own human story."

"Wait, so they can only go to the Ball if they are human? I thought Jane said she saw animals at the Ball too. Was she invited because she was human?"

"Of course they can go to the Ball as animals. The world is full of them, is it not? And who said anything about Jane being a human?"

"Yeah," said Smithson. "She was a crocodile."

"Crocodile?" said Morrow. "That's not how I heard it. She was a rhinoceros!"

"Animals can be more human than many humans, and vice versa," explained Smithson.

"Enough!" Tracey pleaded. "I am on myth overload and will need to digest this for a long time. For now, though, I still don't feel the magical power to conjure up a rift generator."

"Not conjure," corrected Morrow, "but dream. And not in the sense of sleeping dreaming, but weaving into reality without conscious effort. More like unspoken praying. Let the power of the story transform the universe, because the universe is itself the story."

"Well ok then," Tracey said with a terse smile, frustrated. "Why not stop with a rift generator, why not just 'story the universe' into having my kids come back without having to go find them too?"

"Now you get it!" said Smithson.

Tracey snorted. "Why don't I just call them on my cellphone? They're probably at my house right now."

"Yes, do that!" said Morrow, raising his eyebrows.

Tracey regarded him as though he had actually just told her to call her house and find Jeremy and Chris there with a rift generator. She fussed around the room, looking for her purse. An icy feeling gripped her stomach with the thought that she would call her house and they might actually answer. She found her purse and fished out the phone.

"I'm calling right now," she said, voice wavering.

"Good!" said Smithson, cheerfully smiling.

She dialed her home number. It rang three times.

"Uh—hello?" said Chris' voice.

Tracey stammered.

"Ma? Is that you? Jeremy and Cornish Bob are coming soon; they are hiding the ship in the woods for now. Where are you?"

Tracey fainted.

—12—

Ron and Strong stood at the dark maw of the entrance to the extensive cave system inside Underdreck Mountain. They had passed through the Forest of Sighs and the other regions of Dragon Throne World after traversing Historical Mythical Chinese History World, Neverland, and a corner of Oz to get there.

"Tell me again what is in this cave that we have crossed all creation for?" asked Strong.

"I have spent countless hours playing Dragon Throne and know every treasure reward for every side quest. In this cave is the penultimate treasure for the King Ermer story line: the Dreamwalker Helm."

"Ok. And what does one get once one has attained this artifact?"

"One gets the ability to see into another's dreams."

"Oh I get it. So maybe you can wear the helmet and walk through the Dream Plains and see into the whirlwinds without jumping in them. Very clever. But if Dragon Throne is like any other video game, and I've played quite a few, you are going to have a boss fight in order for it to drop. Am I correct?"

Ron pursed his lips. "Sure. I think so, but I don't remember which one it is. I'm sure we can take him, though."

Strong snorted. "I wish I could share your confidence! You don't remember who it is?"

"Oh come on—even though it is a major boss, I'm a high-level character. I could beat any boss but a team dungeon level master-boss without even switching to my back-bar abilities."

"Dude, you don't even have front-bar abilities! What the hell are you thinking?"

"How quickly you forget, Strong. I still have the Men in Black gun."

"I thought you gave that thing to the soul vampire back at the Gnome Mountain siege! Ok, we are good."

Ron produced the small gun from his pocket, and they walked confidently into the mouth of the cave. After a short time climbing down the cave pathway, they saw two goblins lurking in the tunnel ahead. They proceeded more cautiously in their approach. The goblins caught sight of them, and one of them let forth a war whoop and charged. Ron let fly the energy bolt from the Men in Black gun, and the goblin's charred skeleton and what was left of his armor clanked smoking to the stone floor. The other goblin, to their surprise, did not flee. Instead he too charged them, a look of terror plastered on his face. This goblin's war cry sounded more like a shriek of fear. Ron fired again, and the second goblin was fried out of existence.

"Dude! Why did he charge instead of run away?" asked Strong.

"I think they are just programmed to attack in the game. They probably just felt compelled to charge, against their better judgment. That poor goblin! He had no choice but to come at us, knowing he was going to get incinerated! God, this is horrible. We have a bunch more goblins to get through before the boss fight."

"Let's just get this over with," said Strong shrugging. "They will respawn."

They passed through the cave, burning down goblins as they went, until they came to a large chamber with smoking cauldrons flanking a raised dais. A large goblin with more elaborate armor waited endlessly for players to arrive and challenge him.

"Hey, big goblin," called Ron, "why don't you just give us the Dreamwalker Helmet without us having to kill you?"

"I wish I could," said the boss in his gravelly voice, a look of resigned hopelessness in his eyes. "But I have no choice. I am trapped here forever, compelled to fight player characters, get killed, and respawn."

"Not forever," comforted Strong. "Someday, players will stop playing this game, and you can drop from existence."

"Oh thank you very much," the big goblin said sarcastically. "That is so comforting, asshole." With a mighty roar, he raised his double-bladed great axe and charged. Ron fried him.

"Let's get the helmet and scoot before he respawns," said Strong. They found the chest without too much searching around, opened it, and retrieved a horned metal helmet.

"Now we have to get back to the Dream Plains," said Ron.

"Does this game have some kind of 'Boots of Teleportation'? Flying carpet? Instant travel shrines, something like that?"

"They do have wells where you can jump in and appear at another well on the map, but only within Dragon Throne World. We can get close to the edge of the world that way, but not all the way to the plains."

They left the cave, thankfully before the other goblins respawned. A short hike led them to a jump well, but Ron paused before jumping in.

"What is it?" asked Strong.

"I dunno—I am not sure this is going to work. Do you remember how many whirlwinds there were on the Dream Plains? How big that area was?"

"Yeah. I told you before this wasn't a great idea. Even if by some miracle you find her, what if she forgets the dream when she wakes up? Even if she remembers it and builds the rift generator, how will she find the gold ball thing to power it? Remember, we went over this? I told you this wasn't going to work."

"Then why did you come all the way here with me if it was all a waste of time?"

"It wasn't a *waste* of time. I was *spending* time with you, my friend. And time is cheap here."

Ron sat down on the edge of the jump well.

"Look, Ron, you might as well enjoy yourself while you're here. Someday Tracey might find you by some miracle, who knows. But let's go play in the meantime, since there is *absolutely nothing else you can do.*"

Ron pondered. He pursed his lips, tilted his head, and nodded.

"That's my boy," Strong congratulated.

"Ok, here is a compromise. If Tracey is going to find us, we need to be in a place where she is going to look. And with the infinite number of places she will have to choose from, she will have to start looking for me at a place where she thinks I might be. And given her knowledge of me, she will likely start looking for me right here, in Dragon Throne World. And where in this world would she start looking but the capital city of Zijin?

So we will travel to the main square of Zijin and wait for her to find us."

"Uh—wait for how long?"

"Oh, if it is going to happen at all, by her jumping there, it shouldn't take us more than five minutes for her to show up. I mean she has to figure I will be there, and she will just jump right there at that time. So if she doesn't show right up, we can just assume she isn't coming, and we can decide something else."

Strong regarded him sideways. "I'm not sure I follow your logic, buddy, but hey, let's go."

They jumped into the well and clambered out of another well in Zijin. They were in a bustling marketplace, with dusty stone pavings, adobe buildings, merchants hawking their wares, and crowds of robed and armored Dragon Throne denizens milling about.

"Now what?" asked Strong.

"We wait for Tracey. She should come flying up any minute.

They waited. Tracey did not appear. A man in red robes and a piebald horse asked if they wanted to make some gold. They refused his quest.

"So now what?" asked Strong.

Ron Puzzled. "Maybe if I put on the Dreamwalker Helm? Maybe she is in orbit sleeping."

Strong rolled his eyes. "Come on, man, let's go to Lankhmar."

Ron put the helmet on his head. Immediately, he saw the ghostly outline of the bridge of the Glow of Power, the transport ship piloted by Cornish Bob. He saw Jeremy, Chris, Smithson, and, dozing off, Tracey.

"Hey!" Ron shouted. "Come get me!"

*****

Tracey jumped, ripped out of her nap.

"What the *hell*!" Cornish Bob growled, grabbing the ship's controls with one hand and his pistol with the other. They spun around to see a ghostly man with a cartoonishly large horned helmet hovering in their midst.

"Who the flippin' floo are you?" howled Cornish Bob.

"It's me, Ron!"

"What the heck is that helmet?" asked Chris.

"It's the Dreamwalker Helm—never mind. Just come get me!"

"Where are you, Ron?" asked Tracey.

"I'm in the main bazaar in Zijin. In Dragon Throne World!"

"Where the hell is that?" asked Bob.

"Funny you should mention Hell," said Ron. "Hey, is that Cornish Bob?"

"I know where that is," said Jeremy. "I've played that game a few times. Where is that from space, though? We've been floating up here for a few days and—we had no idea how to jump to where you are."

"It's that big world line that goes alongside ours. The one Strong and I were looking at for so long. Open up the rift generator screen. Just jump there; Bob can help you. Find Dragonclaw Mountain," Ron said. "It looks like a giant...dragon claw. Then go west."

"We'll find you. Just stay tight," Tracy reassured.

*****

"Dude, I can't believe that worked."

"I—me too!"

"So you're going to go back?"

Ron sat down on the edge of the dusty well. A monkey in a fez carrying an orange ran by, chased by a shopkeeper.

"I have to. I have a real life back there."

Strong nodded. "Yeah, I get it. I don't. Not much of one anyway. I probably would have chosen to stay here even if I didn't have to by way of dying."

"Sorry about all this," said Ron, clasping Strong on the shoulder.

"*Sorry?* Why sorry, man? Shoot, I'm going to be here for a million years, if I don't get tired. I can always quit if I do. But you know what I'm going to do first? I'm going to learn how to fly. To fly! Then I'm going to become a wizard."

"Then?"

Strong pursed his lips, eyes narrowed. "I'm gonna pull a *Kwai Chang Caine* and wander the Earth. Or the Hell. Whatever."

"Well this is goodbye, then," said Ron. "I have a feeling we will see each other again someday."

"Not in this world, but the next!" said Strong with a grin.

They scanned the skies for any sign of a fiery reentry. There was none. Minutes passed.

"Any time now, Tracey!" said Ron.

"She vill not be coming," said a voice near their knees.

Ron and Strong nearly jumped out of their skins. It was one of the lawn gnomes, the one with the German accent.

"She has been arrested. So has her son and daughter, and your great grandfather. And the long missing escapee, Eiffelia."

They stared at the gnome, dumbfounded.

"And their ship has been impounded. You vill now accompany me for trial."

Ron and Strong silently regarded the gnome, then each other. They shrugged in unison, acknowledging that they had no other options.

The gnome led them through the dusty streets to a nondescript wooden door. He indicated that they enter.

Ron and Strong did and found themselves in a dripping stone-walled jail cell, complete with thick iron bars. They turned back to the wooden door but it had vanished.

Their eyes accustomed themselves to the dim, and Ron saw Tracey, Chris, Jeremy, and Cornish Bob seated around a rough-hewn oaken table on rustic wooden chairs. Crouched in a corner was a small, pale woman Ron did not immediately recognize. There were several flying pickles lazily circling the air.

"Tracey!" Ron squeaked breathlessly.

They embraced tightly, Tracey with a worried expression.

"What happened?" asked Strong.

"I'll tell you what happened, me bey," Cornish Bob drawled. "We dropped out of the jump and had just started plotting a course to your teasey Dragon Dong Mountain. These flying pickles showed up, which should have given us some warning. Then one of those red-hatted dwarf bastards appeared on the bridge. I tried to jump us out of there, but the little bugger had pinched our rift drive!"

"Yeah, they did that to us too," said Ron with a pained look. "Who's that over in the corner?"

"That, my dear, is Eiffelia," Tracey said with a dagger glance. "She was our other surprise. Once the ship dropped back into her old universe, the little chunk of sponge that Bob had broken off back at her planet reconstituted into her real form."

"Good thing I had taken it out of me pocket!" chuckled Bob.

"And he wasted no time in taking advantage of the situation," said Jeremy.

"How's that?"

"I shot her in the forehead," said Cornish Bob.

"That wouldn't kill her here, man. This is Hell," said Strong.

"Yeah, so we found out. Made a mess of the bridge, but she healed up."

"Anyway," continued Tracey with a grimace, "the little gnome guy said we were under arrest for possession of an unauthorized rift device, and we were suddenly here. Awaiting trial. Or something."

"Trial? For what?"

"Like Mom said, possession of an unauthorized rift drive," said Chris. "We told him that your professor friend was a bit more of an offender in that regard and that he was about to blow up half the universe to try to kill baldy over there in the corner."

Ron held up his hand, scrunching his eyes shut.

"Ok. Slow down. Fill me in on what is going on."

They all started talking at once, until Tracey slapped her hand on the table.

"Allow me," she said in the resulting silence. She took a deep breath, put her hands in her lap. "You handed your rift drive to Professor LaGrue. He is intelligent, but mentally unstable, and has only his interests at heart. He exploited the inherent ability of the rift generators by the holder to make unlimited copies of themselves, then returned the original one to you so you and Strong could make the trip to Hell. LaGrue, meanwhile, used the multitudes of his clones and the rift generators each of them held to contend with Eiffelia for control of the universe lines. Then Smithson had a talk with him. To LaGrue's credit, he was convinced that his course of action was leading to widespread misery and pain, including his own. To his detriment, though, his solution to this problem was to blow up as many outposts of Eiffelia as he knew about by driving the rift generators into the systems' stars, causing them to supernova. So right now there are hundreds, if not thousands of stars about to blow, taking the LaGrues, and however many planets full of human or nonhuman slaves out with them. And instead of stopping them, we are trapped here in this stone cell construct in Otherwhen."

"You mean that war that we were watching Eiffelia fight? The Demons? The crashed spaceship? The recruiting soldiers on tv with commercials for giant foam penises? That was all against PeeWee?"

Tracey nodded.

"And your kids? What happened to them?" Ron asked.

"Jeremy and Chris are resourceful and managed to get away from her by stealing this ship. Which Bob in turn stole."

Ron blinked, taking it in. "So what is the deal with her being here?" he asked, thumb pointing over his shoulder at the small, bald woman in the corner who had been identified as Eiffelia.

"From what I have learned, she was originally from here. She escaped with the original rift generator long, long ago, and has managed to avoid coming back here in all those millions of years. Now that a piece of her has been returned, she reconstituted from her sponge form to her original body, apparently."

"So what happened to the rest of her, back in our universes?" asked Ron.

Cornish Bob leaned forward attentively. "Ask her," he said with guarded hostility.

Ron walked to the corner and regarded Eiffelia. She sat in the corner on the floor, knees to her chest, the top of her bald head trembling. She was dressed in an oversized borrowed pair of papery pants and shirt they had found in the ship storage.

"So here you are," said Ron quietly. She said nothing, tears ran down her cheeks.

"Is this all of you? Or are you still in sponge form back home?" he asked.

Eiffelia shook her head. "I'm all here. I'm back." Her voice was the same, in spite of her new looks.

"Well ain't that just fascinating," growled Cornish Bob. "If I had known I could get rid of you so easily by taking a smear o' you back to 'ell, I'd a done that years ago."

"No wonder she didn't tell you, then," said Strong. "The surprising thing is that you never thought to try."

"You shut the feck up, nerd bey, or you'll be waiting for an hour for the innards of yer brain pan to crawl back together."

"Calm down, Bob," said Tracey. "Now what happens with all those LaGrues who are about to bomb stars for no reason anymore?"

A section of the wet stone wall transformed into a wooden door and opened. Professor Langston LaGrue walked through, dressed in a dashing space uniform.

"Well, speak of the Devil," said Strong.

"Hello," LaGrue said as they stared at him. "They said it was time for me to enter the trial."

"Who is 'they?'" asked Ron. "And what do you mean 'enter the trial'—you mean it is going on right now?"

"Yes, it has been going for some time now. For a long time, actually. As far as who 'they' are, it is the Gnomes and the Mods."

"The Mods?" asked Tracey, suddenly inexplicably terrified.

"Yes. We met them before, at that meeting in Seattle. Mr. Barman and Ms. Duma, if you might recall."

"Oh, right. The old guy and the schoolmarm," said Tracy, immediately thinking better of her verbal description with a glance at the flying pickles.

"So what are you doing here now?" asked Jeremy. "Can you get word back to all the rest of you to stop your attacks on Eiffelia's systems? She's not there anymore, you know. She's over in the corner."

LaGrue nodded. "Yes, of course. Already done. As I was strapped in the bridge of my ship, waiting for the order to dive into the sun, one of my other manifestations appeared on the screen with a little being in a red hat, and they announced that Eiffelia was gone. The war was over. We were ordered to report to this universe line, which we did. All of our rift generators were surrendered to the Gnomes."

"What happened to all of you?" asked Tracey. "You LaGrues, I mean."

"We have been judged," LaGrue answered, suddenly somber.

"How?" asked Ron.

"For the crime of theft of a rift generator, for use of that rift generator to propagate myself selfishly, establish a universal scale civilization devoted entirely to myself and my power, and wage war against another such power across time and space, costing millions of lives and endless suffering, my fate is to be left here in Hell until such time as I am allowed to escape. We LaGrues have started off being assigned as the clone stormtrooper army."

"Dude, that is *awesome*," said Strong.

"You don't understand, Jack. It is anything but awesome."

Strong threw up his hands. "Of course it is. You get to play forever. For as long as you want, anyway. You get to develop yourself, learn wizardry, magic, superpowers! No limits, man!"

"There are limits," said a little voice from the corner.

They all turned to look at Eiffelia.

She took a ragged breath and raised her face from her knees where she sat in the corner.

"It's why I left to begin with. Sure, it sounds fun, but only so long as you don't mind losing all the time. I tried to compete in the war zone, but got killed, and killed, and killed. People cheat, you know! They sneak weapons into the no-weapon zone and illegal weapons into the restricted areas. And when you try to protest, they don't listen and don't care. I tried some of the voluntary no-magic no-superpower worlds, but people always cheat there too. It was always 'Oh look at me, I'm a superhero among the mundanes!' so those broke down too. And it was not just the cheating: It was the fabric of the worlds themselves. They were created by people. The player characters, not the programmer of the other world. The operating system was limited, the granularity much more pixelated. Sure, you could fly if you learned the spell or power, but you couldn't pick up every coffee cup! Some places you could climb a ladder, some not! You could go to sleep with a yellow sun and wake up with a blue one! Go for a week farming carrots as a serf and then get fried from orbit by a neutron beam and wake up getting chased by dinosaurs. No continuity, no predictability. It was maddening!"

"So you decided to sneak into our world and be the only one who could cheat," said Tracey, shaking her head.

"Yes. And I'd do it again. I *will* do it again!"

"I don't think so," said LaGrue quietly. "The judgment comes."

The damp stone walls and iron bars of their prison cell grew hazy, then faded into darkness. Out of the dark haze came wood-paneled walls, benches, and a raised dais with a heavy, carved desk. One wall had dirty glass windows, with sunbeams streaming through that illuminated motes of dust and warmed the place uncomfortably. It was a courtroom.

Seated at tables before the dias were Mr. Barman and Ms. Duma. Tracey recognized them from a meeting, seemingly so long ago, in Seattle after Cornish Bob had shot up the town chasing them. Barman was still the dapper balding man wearing his gray suit and tie. His round glasses perched on the tip of his nose. Duma was in the same blue, over-tight dress and apparently still hadn't time to arrange her hair and make-up. It occurred to Tracey that they were still trying too hard to imitate the appearance of humans. They stood.

"All rise," announced Barman. "Court is now in session, the Honorable Arch-Gnome Azaci presiding."

A two-foot-tall gnome with red hat and white beard seated himself on a very tall stool before the head table. The gnome slowly surveyed the scene and made eye contact with each one present except for Eiffelia, who looked away. He produced a long, clay pipe, stuffed it patiently, lit it, and took a few puffs in the silent courtroom.

"Let's begin," he intoned in a reedy voice that carried to the far corners of the courtroom. "Start with the escapee."

"Yes," said Barman, adjusting his round glasses. "The prosecution calls for harsh punishment. Hell had procedures in place for those who wished to emigrate to the mundane world, starting over fresh with a clean slate and no powers. You, Eiffelia, chose to ignore them. You chose instead to steal a rift generator from this august body of duly appointed guardians of the pathway between the worlds. You had planned your unauthorized escape well, inserting yourself billions of years into the past as a lifeform that was virtually immortal, limited only by being forced to control your minions to do your physical will. You failed to maintain adequate safeguards on the rift generator, allowing one to fall into the hands of someone not in your control. As a direct consequence, war on a grand scale ensued and many lives were lost. The grand balance was overturned. All because of your toxic ego. Prosecution recommends that Eiffelia be granted her wish and be placed back into the mundane universe, but as a normal human with her knowledge but no powers. She will then live out the remainder of her life pondering what she has done and what she has lost."

"Defense argues instead that she be left here in Hell," said Ms. Duma. "Her original entry into existence was in this venue. This was her choice, her bargain, her learning path. Why reward her for breaking the grand balance? Return her to her chosen fate here. Give her the chance to learn what she was intended to, or continue her suffering."

Arch-Gnome Azaci pondered, rubbing his bearded chin. He took a long puff from his pipe and exhaled a thin blue smoke stream.

"Her original insertion into this reality stands. Hell it is," he ruled.

"No!" cried Eiffelia. She vanished.

"Whoa!" whispered Strong.

"Next we turn to Strong," said the Arch-Gnome, pointing the stem of his pipe at him. "Arguments!"

"Prosecution recommends, given your prior ruling, that he be returned to his life on Earth. Like Eiffelia, he chose to be born there. And while he did manage to make his way here to hell, and would prefer to stay here—"

"Very much prefer!" interrupted Strong.

"—Prosecution would argue that the methods used were not the traditional ones, and his path would still be best served as his bargain was originally entered into."

"Defense disagrees," said Ms. Duma. "There was no fixed way to make one's way here historically. Transferors could use caves, sea journeys, mind-altering substances, shamanism, and a whole host of other methods to come here. His method is original, but no less valid. He has expressed his desire to play in this set of game rules, and has managed to make his way here."

"While that is true," said the Arch-Gnome, "his original choice carries weight. I see no overriding reason to allow him to make the change at this point, in spite of his technical accomplishment of traveling here. I note by way of dicta that there is precedent for this: Many who have made their way here have either chosen to return or were forced to. You have more to learn there, Jack Strong, before knowingly being able to choose this venue. Back to your life on Earth with you, with only a vague impression of what happened here."

Strong opened his mouth to protest, but a withering glance from the Arch-Gnome silenced him. Strong walked to the back of the courtroom and sat on a bench, head in his hands. He then vanished.

The Arch-Gnome waved the stem of his pipe back and forth between Duma and Barman. "Do either of you have any strong arguments about the fate of Jeremy and Chris, before I sentence them also to be returned to their lives on Earth with no memories of their various adventures?"

"None," said Barman.

"Other than allowing them to retain their memories, none," added Duma.

"Very well, but only vague feelings. No specifics that would compromise the great sundering."

Chris and Jeremy retreated to the back of the courtroom, thinking better of saying anything. They vanished.

The Arch-Gnome surveyed the room. "Let's see...LaGrue we have already sentenced. Tracey Springs is next."

She started in alarm.

"Fear not, Springs. You have done well. Carry on."

"Carry on with what?" she whispered. Ron and Tracey both waited for her to vanish, but she remained.

The Arch Gnome ignored her, chewing on his pipe stem. "Who is next? Ah yes, of course. Mr. Cornish Bob Golden."

"Objection!" Cornish Bob howled. "This court has no jurisdiction! There was an improper arrest, against my rights! Inadequate counsel! Lack of specificity in the charges! This is a travesty!"

"Silence!" thundered the Arch Gnome, rapping his clay pipe sharply on the podium. It promptly cracked.

"Damnit!" he hissed, narrowing his eyes into slits. He took a deep breath and laid the pipe aside. "Arguments," he asked.

"Prosecution calls for harsh sentencing," said Barman. "Golden willingly went into service for Eiffelia, carrying out her pogrom of murder and domination on a galactic scale for her and his own personal ends. He then betrayed her when his own interests served, and instead of returning the rift generator to its proper source, he handed it off to Ron Golden, who further abused its use. His immediate resort to violence, bullying, and ego-selfishness at every turn is the definition of evil, and deserves the full weight of this Court's punishment."

"Defense disagrees," said Duma. "Golden indeed did all these things, but defense calls the Court to consider the deeper magic. His behavior, while abhorrent, made for good Story."

The Arch Gnome raised an eyebrow. "An interesting argument. And well taken. Cornish Bob Golden, your sentence is to be returned to your old life in Bodie. You will be placed one minute before the explosion that you were told caused the rift that allowed you to meet Eiffelia. This rift, unbeknownst to you, was not naturally occurring, but a result of you placing it there at some point in the future using the stolen rift generator by orders of Eiffelia. You will still investigate the results of the explosion, but this time find nothing and live out the rest of your life as originally intended, never knowing or ever finding the additional rift generator you have hidden in the nearby environs of Bodie. This is because you will never think to look for it, and also because I am assigning a Trident agent to recover it. Go now and live your story conventionally as you originally agreed."

"Objec—" he cried, then vanished mid-word.

The Court breathed in the resultant silence for long moments.

"And now we turn to sentencing the main defendant," said Arch-Gnome Azaci.

Tracey and Ron looked around, wondering who was left. Ron was the only one.

"Who, me?" he said in a little voice.

"What did he do?" asked Tracey. Realization then dawned on Tracey's face.

"Yours was the worst offense, the unforgivable crime," said Barman. "You gave your rift generator to LaGrue, because you didn't care or think. You didn't realize the danger of the thing, what it was capable of, beyond just taking you on an interesting adventure to satisfy your curiosity. Or making a buck. His offense was selfishness with knowledge, yours was selfishness from not having your head in the Game. Because of your thoughtlessness, millions of people suffered. This suffering, if caused intentionally, as LaGrue and Eiffelia have done, is not as bad as your causing it from foolishness. Their sin at least contributed to the fabric of the story of the universe. Long ago you chose to be here in this world, like everyone else, to learn and to love. You have learned very little of this. You have spent your life floating along, reacting to things, not making the right effort to engage in the Great Story. You do not give people the proper regard or love. You have been focused on your own ego, your experiences and desires. We are all, in essence, not of this world, but we should be in it while we are here. You have wasted your time out of, well, *laziness*. Your contribution to the story of the world has been puny, in spite of your talents. There are finite and infinite games. While you are in the finite one you should play it, along with the other participants. That is the spirit of things, the Holy Spirit. And offense against the Holy Spirit is unforgivable."

There was silence. A tear ran down Ron's cheek.

"There there," said Ms. Duma. "It is not all bad. You were polite and good. You saved that fellow's job when they wanted to fire him at the factory. You washed the dishes, opened doors for people, watered the plants sometimes. And best of all, you allowed others to rise to the occasion and show their true colors."

Ron opened his mouth, but nothing came out because of the lump in his throat. He closed it.

"But all in all, that accounts for little," said Arch Gnome Azaci. "So now your sentence. It is my duty to administer it."

Arch-Gnome Azaci slid off his bench and tottered on his little legs across the courtroom to Ron. He beckoned with one hand and cupped his mouth with the other, like he wanted to whisper in Ron's ear. Ron bent down and tilted his head to listen. The gnome touched Ron on the forehead with his index finger. Ron slumped to the floor like a sack of potatoes, dead.

—EPILOGUE—

"Thanks for making coffee this time instead of tea," said Maurice. "I'm not such a fan of tea."

"You had but to ask," replied Tracey, pouring into Ron's old Dragon Throne mug. "Cream or sugar?"

"A bit of both, please," Maurice asked.

They sat sipping in silence for a while.

"The funeral was nice," he said. "Good thinking on the urn: no questions about the lack of a body."

She shrugged. "The kids bought it, the whole cancer coming back with a vengeance thing. I have a question, though. You're...dead, right? Burned at the stake and all?"

"Yes."

"Yet you are here, in flesh when you want. And Ron said that his dad had appeared to him as a ghost when he was down in the deep trench base."

"You are wondering whether Ron will haunt you. I suppose it is a possibility. He hasn't appeared to you yet, I presume?"

"No."

"I doubt he will. We Trident types have reason to be here, to come back. Him not so much. You see, once the ball is done, or the video game played, this whole lifetime is like a DVR movie that goes back on the shelf. Later you can play it back, and even re-insert yourself and rewrite the ending. But for what purpose? You and Ron, and everyone else you have ever met, are beyond time and together at this very moment in the real world. You might every now and then dust off the video and re-watch it, but why not just do another movie, another game? Or live there for a while instead?"

Tracey thought about this for a while, sipping her coffee. "So what's next?"

"What's next with what?"

"You know, with the Trident thing. What's the next mission?"

"You want *another* mission? Wasn't going back in time to Bodie without a rift generator merely by the power of your dreaming, recovering a contraband inter-dimensional artifact, and returning it to Hell enough for a while?

"Well when you put it that way it sounds...."

"Sounds what?"

"Sounds like a big deal, but it wasn't."

Maurice raised his eyebrows for a moment. "For now, you go back to work at the Aquarium and stand by. There may be no other missions for a while, now that the war is over and things have quieted down. But you never know."

"Ok. Sounds a bit boring, is all."

"Whatever happened to just living your life, taking out the trash, and all that?"

"You're right, of course. Just seems a bit different under the circumstances."

"Well you never know what will show up at your door."

The doorbell rang. Tracey shook her head at Maurice, who shrugged.

It was Jeremy, still on leave for the funeral, and Chris. They hugged.

"Hi, Ma. They asked us to drop by with some of the leftover food from the funeral. How are you holding up?" asked Jeremy.

"I'm good. Just what I need, a pile of fried chicken. Come in and join Maurice and I for some coffee."

"Hi, Maurice," said Chris. "I still feel like I know you from somewhere. Were you ever on the UW campus? Student or professor or something? Or are you from around here at least, and do we shop at the same grocery store or something?"

Mauriced laughed. "No, nothing like that. We might have met in Otherwhen, but who knows."

"He's just an old friend of Ron's," Tracey explained. "Any number of them might be dropping by while they're in town."

The doorbell rang again.

"I'll get it," said Chris.

Moments later she returned with a rotund bald Hawaiian man.

"Why if it isn't Mr. Morrow, as I live and breathe!" said Maurice.

Tracey snorted her coffee, stifling a laugh because Maurice was neither living nor breathing.

"Good afternoon Tracey," Morrow said, shaking off his raincoat.

"I'll make some tea," Tracey offered.

"No need, coffee is fine," said Morrow.

"How do you know each other?" asked Jeremy.

"Mr. Morrow was my...music teacher," Tracey answered.

"Music? Ma, I didn't know you...played the cello?" said Chris, strangely transitioning from not knowing her mother played the instrument to remembering an entire history of her playing one.

"Of course she did—does," said Jeremy, with an odd glance at his sister.

Morrow beamed with pride at his student's feat of instantly acquiring a skill and retroactively changing an entire set of life histories through the power of dreaming.

"Maybe things won't be as quiet as I thought," she thought. She looked around the table at the sometimes disembodied ghost and the former giant scorpion sitting with her children sipping coffee and realized that this was true.

"So I have an ulterior motive in stopping by, beyond checking on you. I—*we*—need your help," said Morrow with a piercing glance over the rim of his mug.

"Oh? What can I do for you?"

Morrow regarded Jeremy and Chris and chose his words carefully. "There are a number of recently—liberated—populations of people who suddenly had their charismatic leader vanish. Their situation is unknown, they are likely rudderless and possibly volatile. It might be a good idea for you to take Smithson and go on some visits to render aid."

"Some kind of cult? Sounds dangerous, Ma," said Jeremy. "I could go with you if it isn't too long or too far. I still have a few days of leave. Where are they Mr. Morrow? Are we talking Puyallup or Portland?"

"The range is a bit longer than that I'm afraid," said Morrow with a flash of a smile. "But fear not, Mr. Smithson is a professional bodyguard and your mother is quite resourceful and capable herself."

"I would be happy to, Mr. Morrow."

"Well there you go," said Maurice. "Life was in no danger of being a boring Story after all."

www.ingramcontent.com/pod-product-compliance
Lightning Source LLC
Chambersburg PA
CBHW032143170626
46808CB00006B/2345